Diminishing Return

Joseph D. Newcomer

FOR SYLVIA, ANDREA, & ARIELLA NOVA

The most amazing people I have ever known.

ACKNOWLEDGMENTS

Without these unique, talented, and beautiful individuals,
it would be impossible to imagine this life not seeming vacant in some way.

For their support of my writing and their friendship, I would like to thank:
William Hetrick, Aron Shaffer, Lee Edmondson, David Johnson, DAJO, TJ,
The Ottenas, TJG, Trevor Huster, Nikki Keller, Jared White, Aubrey Reese,
Zachary Short, Sperry Hutchinson, Stuart Shoen, Sebastien Reyes, Katie Turk,
Dane Lowrey, David Scott, Bev Walker, The Greenwalds, Turkos, McCalls,
Pitkins, Sousaes, Bruinsmas, Ciminos, Wokutches, Zack Colman
& the two greatest loves of my life,
Andrea Greenwald and Ariella Nova Newcomer.

For inspiration and their invaluable artistic contributions to humanity:
Harvey Danger, Sean Nelson, The Rolling Stones, Bill Murray, David Bowie,
Aerosmith, Steven Tyler, Wilco, Jeff Tweedy, INXS, Beck, The Killers,
Brandon Flowers, Lou Reed, R.E.M., Big Star, Peter Gabriel, CHVRCHES,
Queen, Freddie Mercury, Scott Weiland, The Tragically Hip, Brian Wilson,
Simon & Garfunkel, Don McLean, The Clash, James Dean,
Kurt Vonnegut, Sartre, Elie Wiesel,
Pearl Jam, Bruce Springsteen,
& Aron Shaffer.

For their bravery:
Each of you who suffer from depression and anxiety
and who continue to face each day despite it.
Those who we have lost, and those who lost them.
All of you.

Without memory, there is no culture.

Without memory, there would be no civilization,

no society,

no future.

-Elie Wiesel

1. Before the Beginning: The End. The Pause.

All he can look at is the perfectly drawn contrast her crimson lipstick creates against her pleasantly stark, powdered skin and perfect white teeth. She turns as the small crowd clops and shuffles to a slow stop in front of her. The intensity of her manufactured, cheery expression is rivaled by the boy's complete lack of any expression at all.

.   .   .

We so desperately wanted to be part of their cool. It is easy to see how this is all our fault. The reason, the relevancy, all lost by how simple it became to recognize there was something insatiably alluring about the way things, the way people, were.

Entire generations were defined by a handful of iconic symbols that we gave more meaning to than the living, breathing life around us. We were taken by the ideals of their purity and their depravity, it was better than ours, better than what we had turned it all into. The boring plod of what we decided our lives were, could never live up to the idols we created, the brilliance we assigned to them. There was no time to devote to learning to appreciate something new or unique, especially when we were surrounded by time-tested, genuine articles of beauty and genius. We were all obsessed.

Maybe it started around 2016 when it seemed almost every movie that came out was a remake of something that Hollywood knew had already worked. They recycled it and regurgitated it until it was a sickly dumbed-down, ghastly-pale version of itself. Or maybe it was the constant sampling of old music that designed the impetus of the Age of Sentimentalism. God, I, (we), hated when a song came out and everyone loved it even though it was something someone actually wrote forty to fifty years prior. You couldn't even tell people without their dumb eyes rolling, regardless of how obviously it had been ripped off. It happened so often they eventually passed a law in 2030 making it illegal to sue for copyright infringement. The law stated that the human mind is only capable of so many thoughts and that those thoughts are bound to overlap so each and every thought belongs to everyone. That's when it got really bad.

Then someone figured out time travel… Jesus! That's when the world ended.

.   .   .

It had obviously been left on this shelf as a decoration to be subconsciously noticed, to distinguish the room with a subtle classic touch. He eases it down by the mint plastic handle of its propped open case, sliding it closer to him, off of the shelf, and onto the desk below it. The blank page left in the platen sways and settles. His fingers trace along the smooth, glossy right side, around the bottom, and back up to the top left corner. The machine is forged from the thick, shiny gloss of gumballs and old pictures of polished Cadillac Coupe de Villes.

His fingers continue to trace lightly, easily rumbling over the rounded, cartoon-heart-shaped keys. His middle finger sticks to the F key, and he begins to slowly push. The guts of what feels like a giant geared mechanism churning, break into the clap of thunder. He quickly presses two more keys. The satisfying, thick weight of resistance turns the candy-coated machine of streamlined, airtight amazement into a crude, ancient, lumbering tool. Steel axes chop into the paper leaving delicate, curving symbols.

．　　　　．　　　　．

Well... metaphorically, at least for me, it ended. Quite literally though, time stopped. Not the man-invented idea of time, though that actually stopped as well, but the physical reality of time stopped. The Earth stopped spinning, people stopped aging, and nothing happened... Nothing. Time does not go on infinitely. The lack of time is infinite.

I'm explaining this poorly. Maybe a timeline, the way a timeline would have looked before all of this, would be helpful.

2024 - Nostalgia, Inc. goes public.

Nostalgia, Inc. is a company that won't exist when you are reading this. Nostalgia was a global publishing company that had its hand in all forms of entertainment and media, except radio, which won't exist for very much longer either. It was the first completely recycled entertainment company. It bought the rights to old music, television shows, and movies then re-aired the originals or recreated them to suit the modern standards.

2025 - Nostalgia, Inc. becomes the number one source of entertainment. It also releases the IEOD. The Inner Eye Online Database is a device that is exactly what it sounds like. It has a complete catalog of all previously recorded materials fed to it by an entirely autonomous wireless network. It is the new internet on a microscopic particle. This particle is put into the eye with drops and then it attaches itself where the optic nerve meets the brain so even the blind and eyeless can enjoy it. Nostalgia also announces its new campaign to give every human on the planet the IEOD within five years.

2026 - Nearly all entertainment-involved companies begin to reformat to suit the demand for non-original material so their content can be included on the IEOD.

2027 - The music and movie industries are flatlining. Within a year, less than one one-hundredth of a percent of music and movies comes from any source other than recycled entertainment, and even that one one-hundredth of a percent is hardly original and terribly unpopular.

2029 - All professionally released entertainment creation stops after the final live broadcast in which an IEOD is delivered to the last person on Earth who has yet to have the implant.

2030 - Due to countless failed lawsuits from artists, authors, songwriters, etc., the International Government, the planet's universal governing body, passes the Public Domain of Consciousness Act, disallowing copyright infringement suits of any kind. There is very little public backlash due to the poor quality of non-non-original entertainment.

2032 - Guilford Musso figures out time travel by accident when there is a glitch in his IEOD. The glitch skipped back and forth between two lectures on theoretical time travel and a sitcom (you don't want to know which one), and somehow it spelled out exactly how to travel to the past. He borrows ideas from several old movies and past theoretical scientists to create a time machine that allows for time travel from the present to any point in the past and then back to the present. The machine is less expensive than what an average bicycle would have cost in 2015.

Within six months, the technology needed for time travel is turned into a simple program that can be instantaneously uploaded to any person's IEOD. The upload re-programs neurological pathways to allow for time travel with a simple thought. "Don't just watch the past... Experience the past." That was the new IEOD slogan. One week after the program is released, the IEOD system is hacked and the "Time Experience" program is uploaded into the brain of every living person.

2034 - Due to the overwhelming popularity of past eras' cultures and styles most people spend very little time in the present.

.   .   .

He sits motionless for what feels like a few moments to him, breathing only out of habit. This would be days according to the way his old life feels it, but only a few beats in his current perception. If he hadn't seen the marker of the Vintage Nightly News ghosting over the keys for the third time he would have no way of knowing how long it should have seemed. It is satisfying to see the letters and words and paragraphs which, before he sat down, did not exist. Even in his haziest memory, he cannot recall something this beautiful and hypnotic.

The nightly news comes on again, it's Tuesday. He stands up from the desk and typewriter. The news ends, not that he pays any attention to it whatsoever, but the translucent video watermarks his entire world. *Chick... Chick... Chick... Zip... Ding...* echoes through his mind and he feels one corner of his mouth drift slightly upward into something that could possibly be construed as a grin.

He walks across the twenty-first-floor office (Wednesday) and by the time he reaches (Thursday) the bay windows overlooking the city it's Friday, but only in his eye. Truly, not a moment has passed. No time has passed for over three hundred years. Staring out at the city, he squats down to pick up a small office cubicle trash can. Against the postcard view of the cityscape, he takes each item out and carefully inspects it using the daylight flooding through the window. After inspection, he leaves a battery and an apple core in the wastebasket, and he walks across the room to a large blue can with a recycling label on the side. He drops a handful of papers and a plastic bottle into the rubber can and slides two paper clips into his jacket's chest pocket.

The straps of a sagging black backpack slide off of his shoulders. The bag pivots between his thumb and forefinger, swings around his body, and in one slow, fluid movement, he kicks the bag into the corner. With his back against the wall, he lets his body slide down to the floor. He leans into the corner shadowed behind the recycling bin. His head touches his bag just as his eyes close.

.   .   .

In the following couple of years, the side effects of time travel become increasingly evident. I think the first effect that was impossible to foresee or imagine was the literal end of "society" as we knew it. Cities and towns, in the common understanding of them, cease to exist. People begin living in the eras of their choosing, sometimes hopping back and forth like they are channel surfing. There is no longer even a need to govern the present.

As the use of time travel increases, the present day time starts slowing and the effects of all of this time-traveling become even more inconceivable. At first, it is completely imperceptible because everything slows down at the same rate, but we eventually realize people are no longer aging. All animal and human reproduction begins to fail. Basic human needs, air, water, food, all start to become unnecessary.

.   .   .

This can easily be the still, dead body of a gaunt vagrant. Greasy curls of black hair crawl over his five-day stubble covered cheeks and fall lifelessly onto his bag. A tee-shirt that may have, at one time, been white, folds and twists between the unzipped front of his pea-green, military-style jacket. Frayed denim, worn through to white threads at every imaginable joint, struggle to cover his legs down to his feet where the failing blue material bunches to rest on old, dusty, tan cowboy boots.

This is not sleep. This is pretending. This is pretending that "nothing" isn't happening. With closed eyes, shut off from the catastrophic peace, staring at the back of his garbage can shadowed eyelids and through the dim, ever-present programming, he can feel the only familiar touch of an existence that no longer is, nor can be. This is less than nothing, but it connects him to time, to his past. Even if it is only a placebic effect, with the "nothing" shut out, he can feel something resembling exhaustion satisfying rest.

9

This is more like the nothing he used to know.

The gritty squeak of an office chair startles him to attention.

.   .   .

2038 - Time stops.

It just stops. Time travel is invented and about six years later, which I would guess to be about one hundred and fifty years according to my sense and understanding of time, it just stops. I mean, everything stops. Somehow, we can still move through time and even the paused present, and we are still able to interact with almost everything.

The worst effect of constant time travel, in my opinion, is the loss of memories. Time travel enough and you forget your entire past, or if you chose, you can manually wipe your memory once you arrive at a new time destination to make the experience even more organic. You don't even know you time traveled. Wiping your memory in the past does not completely delete it from your present consciousness, but it does speed up the process of losing your actual memories.

We knew it was happening after a while, but it was too late.

It isn't that no one cared about losing their past, it was just that we couldn't resist going back. Even those who adamantly opposed time travel ended up going back once there was nothing here to keep them.

I'm sure there are tons of questions at this point. I will answer a few. No, interacting with the past does not alter the future, at least not in the way people once perceived that it would, according to movies and TV. Going back to the past and changing something does not affect the present. I couldn't tell you why for sure. I guess the time in which our consciousness resides cannot be altered because it has already occurred. Maybe reality is specific to each individual. I don't know why exactly, but if I go back and cut off my own younger version's finger, for some reason my finger does not fall off or disappear. If I stay in that timeline, I can watch my younger self continue to grow as a person without a finger. I could even cut my current self's finger off while visiting the past, but once I travel through time again, my own reality is restored with all of my digits intact because it happened after the fact of my original existence through time to this point, the paused present.

Some people believe making these changes to the past spurs alternate timelines which splinter off indefinitely, but this isn't the reality of the timeline that we live in, so we could never really understand if that is actually happening. Though whatever you have done, whatever has happened in your time travels simply goes away in your own perception, the memories of these time travel experiences stay, vacating your actual memories in the process. Our minds are full of things that never occurred, simulations of life, abandoned versions of reality.

People can stay in an altered timeline until they die if they choose, but they only die in that timeline. This is another thing the program does to increase the experience of being in the past. When you are there, your body ages naturally. You can have kids and grow old, you can even die of natural causes in the past but since your actual timeline has stopped you don't really die, the program just auto-jumps you to the present. Even if you get hit by a car or eaten by a dinosaur, you still just wake up in the paused present, the same age as when you left, the only difference is maybe you forget grade school or playing little league.

You can live without time, but you cannot die without it. Dying is what makes living worth anything and no one has died according to your time's terms since 2035, which now feels like more than three hundred years ago to me. I figure the three hundred years by counting the number of times a full week's worth of IEOD programming cycles through, during what intrinsically feels like a day to me. I've been letting my IEOD run with 99 percent transparency since shortly after time stopped. I don't really know why. I think it somehow makes me feel connected to how things used to be, but it really isn't an accurate gauge by which to measure anything. I can only, honestly estimate the passing of time with my perception as it exists now. I actually believe the amount of time that has passed based on how you would perceive it would be unimaginable due to the fact that you have never experienced time slowing or stopping. The lowest number of years that I could come up with, based only on things I know with absolute certainty, is eight hundred sixty-four thousand years plus whatever amount of time that would have added up before the Pause, when I started trying to keep track. I say the lowest number because my IEOD programming has been gradually speeding up since the Pause, that or days are getting longer in my perception, maybe both.

With all of that said, it is well beyond my knowledge to be able to even begin to explain, with any sort of accuracy, how to calculate the amount of time that passes for anyone when time itself has stopped. For our purposes, it's been lifetimes. It feels like it's been lifetimes.

While no one has technically died in all of this "time," I rarely see another living person. There is really no reason to come to the present day Pause unless you "die" somewhere in the past. Even when the program auto jumps someone to the present day, almost no one stays for more than a moment. They just go right back to whenever they want. I'm not condemning it. I've done it. We are all recycled people.

Generally, the only time people stick around for more than a few of your minutes is when, what I would consider to be, a real death happens. I think the only real death is when you've time-traveled so much that all of your original memories are deleted. When every last original memory fades away, your IEOD has an explanation program to help you understand what is happening. Once people are given the information, and they find out they can travel through time, they just go right back to doing so with no hesitation.

The process can take a couple of, what you would consider, hours. Their reactions are robotic and hauntingly emotionless. I realize that they made the choice knowing that they would inevitably lose every memory, but I cannot escape feeling their loss in myself when I see it happening. Not everything is wiped away though. You don't forget how to do things, but you do forget how you learned to do those things. It strips away your humanity, your care of why you are the way you are, what happened that made you that way, the people that you knew. Hell, maybe that is what people really wanted--just to forget everything. I can't say that I blame them. I've seen it happen a handful of times. I call them "company" even though we generally have no direct interaction.

The first time I came back to see you, me, I couldn't believe how much more I liked myself when I was younger. My initial thought was probably like everyone else's, "I'll go back and give myself advice to see how shit would have turned out if I just would have…" Fill in the blank. Now I realize what an insanely ridiculous fantasy that is. You thought I was a fucking lunatic. I watched for years just enjoying how you reacted to things, how I used to be before IEODs and all of this shit, before settling into this stillness, before accepting anything at face value for the sake of a little peace and quiet. Ha, peace and quiet, that's all there is now.

Trying to give you advice was a joke. You were staunch in your decisions and opinions. You had better judgment, more passion. You were just a better version of me. You had this amazing rock band and all of these great ideas. You fucked and fucked up all the time. Spoiler alert, you are now a garbage man. It sounds terrible, but once life strips you of your self-involved entitlements and your expectations become realistic, you will actually choose this path and what will sound even more insane to you is that you truly enjoy it.

As you read this, you'll think we settled, but I assure you that while your passions and judgments are fewer and less invigorating, they have also become more directed and can be more satisfying and discerning. You still fuck up constantly, that hasn't changed except that now it means more when you do. Eventually, possibly, at some point, something you read here may help you. I don't think that the present, the future for you, can be entirely avoided. Hell, maybe it can't be avoided at all. I just hope that there is a possibility you could spend more of your time appreciating time while it exists for you.

In actuality, you really haven't been a garbage man for a few centuries and now you miss it terribly. Imagine that! Once time stopped and no one needed to eat or shit or do anything, once there was actually no one even here to eat or shit or do anything, there was no garbage or, to be more accurate, everything in the world is now garbage: anything that no one wants, needs, or uses-- garbage, all of it.

.   .   .

"Holy shit! I know her," he says aloud, though he isn't quite sure if he has or if he just thought the words.

A small older woman has appeared in the cubicle next to the office where he had been using the typewriter. Before the Pause, she used to walk her dog near his apartment. They never spoke in more than half-smiling nods with a 'morning' or 'g'afternoon' but they'd seen each other almost daily for years. It was a very rare occasion that he saw anyone he recognized. This isn't a "real" death. She vanishes before he is able to get to his feet. Still, he walks to where she had been. Next to her seat, the air has the faint smell of talc. He recognizes the smell from when he used to pass her on his old block. He slides the faux wood-grained nameplate out of the holder on the cubicle wall and reads the

16

etched white name aloud.

"Louise Aster."

"G'morning, Louise."

He puts the nameplate back into the aluminum holder and goes back to the typewriter.

.   .   .

Before everything stopped, there was a girl.

.   .   .

"So, you're saying that even though you have a life where you can go back and do whatever the hell you want to do, with no consequences, no worries, no attachments, no one to offend or be offended by, no fucking problems at all, all you want to do is sit here? What happened to you? I come back and you're just sitting around. I mean, why the fuck are you even here?"

"It just seems kind of pointless."

"POINTLESS? It's fucking perfect. You have lost it. I'm

going back."

She looks at him with her eyebrows raised and her mouth slightly open. She waits for the response she is so accustomed to getting from this posture. This time he truly does not, cannot care. He slowly leans over himself, pulls his foot up and over to cross his knee, and starts to pry off his boot. She watches as he calmly struggles for a moment.

Her arms swing back from her body as it lunges and throws the words out of her mouth at his face.

"Fuck you!"

She is gone. He doesn't look to see if she has disappeared, but he knows she has. The boot clumps and half rolls on the floor by the couch and his hands go to work on the other foot.

.   .   .

You know her now, but I won't ruin the surprise for you just in case you actually do end up reading this. The last time you spoke to her in at least three hundred years, you barely had the strength of conviction to look her in the eye. I can't imagine a future where you will speak with her again, at least not a "her" that remembers you. I can't really imagine a future at all. You do share some fantastic years together, but in the end, she goes back and you completely understand. I don't think you knowing the end will change how it plays out, but I would like to imagine it can. I just couldn't bring myself to go back anymore, it wasn't a choice.

She was kind of right about one thing though, a lot about the Pause was pretty ideal. There hasn't been war or crime or hunger since the Pause. Who would have thought that Utopia would happen when there wouldn't be anyone around to notice it? I guess it is pretty obvious that humanity's one true, defining characteristic is imperfection so it is not that shocking that everything is better without us. Nothing, truly, is "perfect." Somehow, I doubt that was what she meant.

.   .   .

Standing up from the desk, he glances again at the windows for a beat and looks back down at the typewriter. He pulls the half-used page from the rollers out of the top of the machine, stacks it with a few type covered pages, and slides them into an opened ream on the desk. He reattaches the suitcase-style, plastic cover over the top of the typewriter and picks it up by the mint handle which desperately hangs on with its corroded, brass hinges. He makes his way to his bag, throws it over his shoulder, and leaves through a door beneath an unlit exit sign. He begins to make his way down a flight of stairs past a large, painted mural that reads "20" in crude, black, block font. His shoulders slump away from his neck as he remembers the walk up the stairs. The door inches open, and he pushes his way out into a city block of open parking lot that is randomly half-filled with several cars. He squints and shades his eyes with his free hand. This lot is a vintage, muscle dream. Every car is an immaculate recreation of an antique American classic. In the corner of the lot, he spots a remake of a Fifties Triumph Trophy Motorcycle which is an exact replica of James Dean's bike. He knew the bike from old pictures that he'd seen. He'd seen it once in person as well, on one of his time jumps. Now, the bike is just trash like everything else.

He makes his way to the motorcycle, takes a rope out of his backpack, and straps the typewriter to the two springs under the seat and the rear wheel cover. The keys are in the ignition where a fake white rabbit foot dangles from a small chain. After three awkward attempts, the engine kicks over, and a thick, black cloud of smoke fires out from behind the bike.

.   .   .

To be honest though, it's nothing even approaching

perfection. Imagine never being hungry or tired… ever. The only thing that wears is your mind or your soul, if that is still a thing or if it ever was. You adopt the perception of gods and cartoon characters. Some of it sounds perfect and amazing but it ends in the purest, absolute narcissism, plagued with a want that is fueled only by itself. Humans need to need and to be needed to be human. Without that intrinsic drive, the only decisions to be made are fleeting whims that eventually bore until everything is unimportant and apathy completely takes hold.

I force myself to keep habits, to fake the need, eat three times in what feels like a day, pretend to sleep through what would be the night, I even "nap" when I can't bear this, but it's all pretend. It's probably no better than living a million fake lives in the past to anyone but me, but regardless of how much of my routine is pretend, this still feels more real to me.

What excruciatingly very little effect my existence has on the Pause, it's better than not having any effect on anything at all. I rummaged through trash, I rode a motorcycle, I fucking recycled. If I were in the past, I couldn't have actually done any of that. The things I'm doing will remain done until, well, forever. If I had traveled back before the Pause and done those things, eventually, I would wake up to find out that the bike had never moved and the can of trash had never been sorted. I would be left only with the phantom memory of things I hadn't actually done. I just can't bear the futility of it all. Pointless, I was a little bit right too.

• • •

2. The Days and Nights

The chugging of a gas-powered, portable generator nearly drowns the crackle and chirp of a campfire and crickets which flit out from the narrow opening of an exit-only, fire escape door. The door is held slightly open by an extension cord coming from the generator and going into the gray cinder block and mortar building. A fourteen-foot U-Haul truck is parked nearby with its back gate left open. The box of the truck is entirely empty with the exception of four large gas cans bungee-corded to the sidewall. The truck's ramp is extended to meet the ground beside a motorcycle leaning on its kickstand. Everything is surrounded by a thin fog of exhaust.

Inside the doorway, the room recesses into the ground and opens up to feel even bigger than the outside. Here, the sounds from the two sides of the door exchange volumes. The white-noise, background whir of the generator can barely be recognized under the campfire cracks and cricket songs which are now punctuated amidst an unmistakable smattering of pops and fuzz that can come only from a vintage record player. The sounds blast into a cathedral echo around the room. In the room, it is night. The massive dome ceiling is disappeared by cosmic blackness littered with stars. The center of the room is nearly pitch-black except for a tiny, directional pin light hovering over a typewriter keyboard which is being intermittently shadowed by hunting and pecking fingers. One of the hands reaches up to the light. With a click, the light is gone, and with it vanishes the last remaining evidence which disproved the room's illusion of a dark world.

.   .   .

A tire iron clangs and bounces against the concrete floor making him jump back even though he had caused the raucous. He stops the door from swinging closed with his hand and bends to pick up the metal tool as he slides into the room. With a shrug of his shoulder, his bag falls around his body and under his arm. He pulls out a flashlight and scans the room. The light traces a chain-link fence to a padlocked gate with a sign that reads "Evidence Locker." He hits the lock with the tire iron five times before it clunks open. Inside the gate, his flashlight pans the shelves covered in cardboard boxes and sealed plastic zip-lock bags. He positions

24

the light on the shelf behind him and places the tire iron back into his bag. With his hands free, he begins opening the bags and boxes one by one, inspecting their contents in the light.

The beam of light through the plastic bag casts the shadow of a gun onto the rack behind it. He pulls at the top of the bag, stretching the plastic taffy until it slowly separates. A silver nine-millimeter shines in the light as he inspects it. The weight and cool of the steel are satisfying against his hand. He pulls a loaded clip from the torn plastic and pushes the clip and the gun into his backpack.

He shuffles a few bags around on the shelf like a psychic shuffling a deck of cards for a reading. The air fills with a skunk musk. He smiles, picks up the flashlight, and holds another bag, this one filled with pot, in the shine of the beam. His eyes quickly glance over his shoulders as he tucks the pot into his bag with the gun and ammo. His caution is an obsolete souvenir from a time when time would have required it.

The beam of light bounces down the aisle to the end of the row and floats over the rest of the room. Shadows sharpen and fade as they race away from the light until it comes to rest on a bag of golf clubs leaning in a corner. His hand reaches out to the bag, singling out a Titleist seven-iron with a dried crimson glaze on the clubhead. He scratches at the fragile, flaking stain and a few red, glassy shards fall through the bright chrome glare reflecting from the shaft of the club.

"Rough day on the links, honey?"

He lets the club sink back into the bag and unzips the oversized, side pocket revealing several dozen, white, dimpled balls. He zips the pocket closed and throws the bag over his shoulder. The light leads him as he leaves the cages. The shelves of derelict evidence sink back into the shadows and out of existence.

.   .   .

"Four!" he screams, breaking the stagnant silence of the abandoned rooftop.

There is a faint clunk of a golf ball hitting the hood of a car as his head points back to the ground. He mutters to himself through a chuckle and the typewriter-paper joint hanging from the corner of his lips.

"Not that it fucking matters."

From the pile spilling out of the golf bag tipped over on the rooftop, the head of the seven iron pulls another ball into the middle of his stance. He readies his grip and squints his left eye to keep the thin stream of smoke from stinging it. He pulls the club back slowly, in an awkwardly amateur motion. With a swift jerk,

26

he brings the clubhead around and strikes the ball off of the roof. He shields his eyes from the sun to follow the ball as it severely hooks into the distance. A tiny explosion of glass echoes back to him.

Intoxicated shouts of "Ha, ha, ha, fuck you!" burst through the city as he throws the club to the side. He holds up both arms with his middle fingers extended. He swings his forearms, gesturing back and forth to no one and nothing. As he steps back, all of his weight shifts to his heels. With his middle fingers still saluting the sky, he allows the chemically induced vertigo to push his body down to the rubber-coated roof. His head bounces off the ground as he continues to laugh until it turns into a chuckle. The chuckle fades to a grin. The grin fades and he closes his eyes.

.   .   .

The apathy creeps in more when inhibitions are low. The boredom is so rarely changed. It doesn't matter how hard you try to avoid it, it's always right there. The animals at the zoo have even lost all pretenses. You can walk into the Polar Bear exhibit and pet the poor bastards. They're alive, their eyes are open, but they just don't give a shit about you or anything else. Sometimes, I want to lie down next to them and just wait for whatever it is that those animals are waiting for.

It's not as if things were great before the Pause either. People's affectations for living with a phone in front of them quickly turned the world into a giant vending machine where no effort was required to obtain anything. Just press a few pretend, touch-screen buttons and get whatever you want. Not even real buttons! We couldn't even be bothered with asserting even the minutest of physical forces to satisfy any single whim. That is why I love this machine with which I write to you. As I press each key, my finger is met with an initial resistance. When that resistance breaks, it gives way to the typebar's short and quickening descent until it stops as it stamps itself to the crisp paper. Then the steel peels back into its place, flourishing and creating in the entire movement, every stroke leaving something that didn't exist before it. It settles a hunger I'd forgotten, or maybe I'd never known at all, but now possesses me.

●　　　　●　　　　●

3. The Dead Girl

Her hair is parted at her right temple with a blurred, spinning bullet. The bullet hangs on nothing, just a fraction of a millimeter away from her chalk and freckle skin. His eyes widen at the realization of her halted self-ending. She seems painfully unaware of nearly everything and her face is mired in concerned confusion that is subdued only by her body's lethargic detachment. He can't be sure, but he doesn't think this is a real death. She lacks the saddened dead look of "company." He stares silently, waiting for her to vanish as he closes the door behind him. The flicker of shows glowing in his eye flash through weeks before he can find the strength to whisper to himself.

"What the fuck? Why are you still here?"

She turns her head and the spinning lead follows, staying completely poised in its proximity to her. It's as if the bullet is an unconnected appendage, now as much a part of her as her curly, thin, red, chin-length hair or her giant, bright, celadon and emerald irises. She wipes away a trickle of blood falling from the corner of her eye. He notices a smoky stain in the white of her eye as her finger passes, tracing over her blushed cheekbone. The stain reminds him of old, burned-out light bulbs. The memory of light bulbs burning out pushes a moment of satisfaction through the disturbed wonder that grips his face.

"How long have I been here?" she asks.

He feels his chest exploding. His throat ties itself into a knot, and he can only gruntingly clear it and wait until it opens so that he can speak. Her voice is clear and heavy and plagued by tired concern. Her words soak into his eardrums collecting behind his tonsils. The warm bath of tone replaces a pressure which he had evolved beyond feeling, but now the sensation of its absence overwhelms him.

He chokes again, "Ah, it's kind of hard to explain."

He feels his words coming out too softly. He is whispering and knows it, but he can't force any more volume through the dry, limp muscles in his neck. He wonders if she hears him. Her eyes are much more focused on the surroundings than where the answer to her question is coming from. With the awkward cautiousness of an abused animal, he moves nearer to her. His body freezes as her eyes meet his.

"What do you remember?"

He believes he has managed to speak loudly enough for her to hear him.

Her head turns away from him for a moment. She visibly strains to recall anything. Her head shakes slightly while her eyes trace back to his. Even though she has come to with a perfect stranger in the room staring at her, somehow, she still appears to be calm.

"I remember feeling that there was something important, a weight under my eyes. It's gone. I don't know what... There's something I'm missing, I'm not supposed to be here, maybe."

Her words build a symphonic pressure in his gut that grips him to her attention. With her voice still wandering through the room, his own words now sound sick and jarring to him.

"I think you live here."

He points at a picture of her on a shelf next to a collection of records. She is much younger in the photo, but it is unmistakably her. The record collection is immense, stretching from wall to wall and ceiling to floor with only a few gaps on the shelves that had been reserved for memorabilia of concerts and framed pictures. He knew the pictures well. He'd come here several times to borrow records since he'd decided to remain in the Pause. Though he'd imagined it during each visit, this is the first time she has appeared and regardless of their countless imagined interactions, he is still unprepared.

She stands and walks to the picture.

"She does look like me," the words drain out of her in a breath of disappointment.

She folds the picture frame down toward herself, onto its face, and out of sight. The disappointment in her voice pulls at his guts, but it also implies that she does remember something. Even if that something she remembers is only that she recalls wanting to forget, it can't be a real death. It is clear that she is completely indifferent about his presence, but he cannot stop his feeling of awkward intrusiveness.

"I can go. I'll go. I will come back later. Sorry, I, I'll go."

Moving past him, she is a ghost. He watches her drift by him, and he wonders if she noticed the bullet in the reflection on the glass of her portrait or if she can feel it hovering next to her. She speaks but makes no attempt to direct it at him. Her tone is now void of any emotion.

"Okay, come back later."

He watches as she leaves the room. He is as careful and silent as death as he opens the dark, thick, stained-wood door and slides out onto the porch. His regret is immediate and defeating.

He peers through the floor to ceiling paned glass windows at the record collection. The room is hash marked by the shadows of the rectangular window frames and the sunlight bleeding through them. She's not there. He continues to stare over his shoulder through the window as he walks away until the house is out of view.

.   .   .

I'm not sure anyone ever actually lived in the present. Before the Pause, and honestly, even now I think we only really live in the past, even if it is only the immediate past. There is a seductive safety in thinking only about things that have already happened. They're concrete. They have a beginning, a middle, and an end. There's no sick anxiety of things that could happen. There's nothing to fear.

We are incapable of processing the present until it is a moment behind, and we can only react a moment too late. Maybe we are never really here, we just always were here. Given the option of terrifying ourselves about what could possibly come or completely isolating ourselves from everyone and everything and drowning in hollow, ineffectual nostalgia where we could neither hurt nor be hurt, we choose the latter.

34

What was the alternative? If we weren't anxiously contemplating the possibilities of the future, reminiscing about the past, or processing the immediate past, I guess we could have said that we were living in the present, but the present is now an empty impossibility. I'm not really sure the present even exists.

Whatever it is, it's not Hell or Purgatory or anything so clearly defined, but it is no less a prison. As people, we generally love our prisons, even if we feign to deny it. We choose them, or we build them, and we accept and appreciate the sad satisfaction of knowing what to expect from them. This present isn't a prison that will give you that satisfaction. We used to champion living within our self-created confines, but this present is a uniquely crafty demon that I can only grind my bloodied fingertips against while clawing at its walls as I try desperately to get inside. Leaving smeared wine handprints and gouges is the only reality for me now. Those grisly reminders of what I've done will be here tomorrow, should tomorrow ever happen. I could no longer convince myself that any other option was anything but the stuff of dreams and make-believe.

I get angry when I consider that this was all a foregone conclusion. If anyone could understand, it would be you. I met a dead girl. She must have shot herself just as the Pause started. I'm not sure if she even knows it's there, but the bullet she must have tried to kill herself with is just waiting for time to start again so it can push through her temple. Here, in the Pause, she could go on being almost dead forever and still function as if nothing has happened. In fact, nothing has happened.

There had to be parts of her that died before she pulled the trigger. I was wrong. This is as close as you get to a real death, at least for now. I understand the desire to give up, I honestly do, but seeing it, watching the bullet spin next to her, it shines a light on the vast difference between having very little to live for and preferring nothing at all.

She may be stuck here. I've rarely seen anyone stay for as long as she did. There have only ever been two other people that I have had full conversations with since I decided to stay in the Pause. From what I can tell, her IEOD may be broken. I've never seen it happen, so I can't be sure. I can't stop wondering if she pulled the trigger before or after it broke.

I am ashamed to admit it, and probably wouldn't if this wasn't only going to be read by you, but either way, whether she tried before or after the IEOD broke, it makes me like her already. Preferring death over the Pause or a never-ending cycle of meaningless episodic existences seems like one of the few sane or rational conclusions to me. Only a truly psychotic person would, given the present circumstances, not, even at the very least, consider it. Maybe this isn't all there will ever be though, and that ever-diminishing touch of hope is enough to hold back. At least for me, it is, for now.

Still, it is heartbreaking to wonder how she may have gotten to this point.

•　　　•　　　•

4. The Planetarium

The door smacks against the outside wall and swings back. She catches it with her back and elbows as it flies back into her body pushing her onto a platform inside the room. The grinding engine noise of the generator floods in with a breeze of exhaust and sulfur. The crash and fumes smack him to the attention of her silhouette in the doorway.

He scrambles to his feet while reaching for the console next to him in the center of the room. His hand finds a slider and the room brightens. She laughs as if she has caught him in the middle of some perverse act. His tense shoulders fall from their spasm into a normal posture. His startled frame relaxes, slumping into mild embarrassment. He laughs with her.

"Sorry if I startled you?"

She busts in like she's robbing the place and then, all of a sudden, she has manners, he thinks.

"I was just reading."

She allows the door to close behind her as she examines the gigantic, domed room. Her jaw shifts back and forth while her mouth holds itself open as if it is waiting for more words to articulate and spill through the small gap in her lips.

He stares up at her. She is different from how he saw her in the record house. Now, as she stands a few feet above him on the wheelchair ramp stage in front of the door, she is commanding in an entirely new way. Now, she is an Eighties pop-punk princess from her silver pumps and skin-tight, torn, black jeans to her washed out "The Clash" t-shirt and heavy, black eyeliner. Hints of unmistakable femininity peek through her purposeful, harsh shell. Her delicate, milk hands are tipped with a glossy, pink shade that matches the color of the fading, silkscreened word "London" running down her torso, just right of her chest. She seems oddly engaging and confident. She holds her wrist against her body at her waist, on her left side, where her elbow and hip jut out leaving all of her hundred and twenty-ish pounds to rest on her left foot. Her right leg and foot are turned out ninety-degrees and appear to be detached from the rest of her.

Had she been tapping her pointy, reflective-chrome pump, she would be the motion picture cliché of the irritated girl impatiently waiting on a gentleman caller. Her posture is a disjointed smattering of sharp angles that make her much grander than her naturally given, tiny frame, not unlike any number of cute, unassuming creatures that distort themselves as a defense mechanism, but also not unlike a predator charading as harmless.

The room is simple and cavernous. Row after empty row of reclining theater seats flood the floor and trail off across the room where they shrink into perspective insignificance. Most of the room is abandoned and untouched except the very center where a projector is perched over a makeshift den complete with a full bookshelf, a dying, beaten, washed-out brown leather couch, a fifties style record player with a cherry wood base and an ornate, brass horn, and a one-piece wooden chair and desk. The desk houses a mint green typewriter which is highlighted by a freestanding, gooseneck, pin spot lamp. Chairs from the center of the room have been removed to make way for the modest living area. A nearly inaudible, arresting hum reverberates from the pale, glowing canopy. Though the hum is not a discernible sound, it applies its steady heft to everything in the room, dampening every other noise with its dense pressure.

Her hand lazily slides against the rail down the ramp. At the bottom of the ramp, she lets her arm fall carelessly from the railing. She crosses her arms behind her back and turns toward the center of the room. Her face leads her while the rest of her body tentatively trails behind. She studies the empty swath of ceiling and perfect rows of chairs. He watches as his view of her switches slowly back and forth between her left and right profile. Once she is in the imaginary confines of his pretend study, she looks directly at him for only a moment in their reality, but in his perception, that moment is played out in an impossible slow motion. She directs her attention more specifically to the items lining his bookshelf. Her fingers drag over each record and book as if she is cataloging the items he may have taken from her home.

He tries to steal himself from the race of thoughts in his mind so that he can conjure some mundane nicety and attempt a conversation. The barrage of thoughts moves nearly as fast as the ghosting images in his eye. His IEOD now seems to be moving faster than ever. He realizes that he has completely lost track of how many cycles have passed. Due to this new distraction, he can't even recall when he stopped paying attention. His throat catches as he tries to swallow the growing lump that forms. He digresses into a swell of worry and fear and begins to mourn the loss of his last connection to time. He sits back, defeated, into the desk chair, and he awkwardly turns away from the typewriter to face her. On the back of his head, his fingers lay tracks through his matted hair as he attempts to soothe the newly aching base of his skull.

He watches as she pulls a record from the shelf. She expertly slides the vinyl out of the cover and places the record on the turntable. Her graceful hand pivots and lowers the brass arm. The needle grinds through the quieting echo of rhythmic clicking wooden blocks and a few sharp guitar notes accented by falsetto shouts, all of which quickly give way to soft static. The needle glides through random pops. The room is held hostage by the suspense of the closest thing to silence that the machine can manage.

The familiar vinyl hiss drags his attention out of his thoughts and back to the girl. She turns away from him and walks to the bookshelf. The quiet static gives way to several lazy measures of jangly slide guitar. Brassy, English-accented vocals stretch out over the music. The words and guitar notes rub right up against the edge of what should be acceptable in this key and then deliberately, expertly they drawl in and out of it. It is beautiful in its entirely imperfect, raw-nerved humanity. He has heard the song before, but he has never paid such close attention.

"Take me to the station and put me on a train."

Her fingers brush across the books again, but this time she sways and her hand dances with the satisfied carefree touch of a child along the titles and spines.

"I've got no expectations to pass through here again."

The smooth motion of her body halts and her face reaches over her shoulder to him. Her eyebrows rise into assumption which he can foresee quickly becoming a defensive scowl if he were to not immediately meet her next words with the same tone of incontrovertible truth in return.

"You do love the Rolling Stones, right?"

Her eyes stay locked on his while her half-smile, half-toothy sneer demands his response. He adjusts his posture to deliver his words with the correct amount of like-minded indignation for why that question would ever need to be asked.

"Yes, of course!"

Her body resumes its easy silken motion, back and forth. Her hips lag behind the beat of the music, punctuating each measure just a beat out of time. She casually nods her head while she returns her attention to the bookcase. Her pale, pink fingernail folds over the binding of a simple leather-bound book. The book tilts as it slides away from the rest, revealing a yellowed ream of pages accented with several paper clips. She pulls the book the rest of the way off of the shelf and quickly tilts a few of the works that neighbor the empty space. Most of the books have at least one space held with a paper clip.

Full, clean piano chords bleed through the rest of the music, filling the hollow room. The thick chorded chorus resonates over everything, even the dampening hum. The tone relaxes the frayed edges of the recording and the muscles in his neck.

She spins and free falls into the corner of the old, catcher's mitt couch. The cushions inflate and rush to envelop her. The inflated beaten material slowly exhales a sweet, stale, comforting breath as the cushions die back into their true limp form.

The book falls open in her lap. She stares downward, her face straining with confusion.

"What's with all the paper clips?"

His entire world is being interrupted. Her scolding, sarcastic voice reminds him of how people interact, how guarded and calculated actions used to have to be to make society work. He cannot remember the last time he felt this way, but the nauseating anxiety of judgment is familiar and comforting. Having to defend his actions is amusing to him.

"I lose interest. The paper clips hold my place."

"There are a lot of paper clips!" her words come out in a forced whisper with more volume than the original question.

The irony isn't lost on him. He knows that her new tone is at his expense. Her mouth hangs open and her brow is still contorted with disbelief.

"Yeah, I always think I will go back to finish, but if I read the end then the story is over. You know?"

She shakes her head, "Don't you want to know what happens? Don't you want that satisfaction, that sense of accomplishing something you started? It would drive me insane to not read the last word so that I could add it to the collection in my brain."

He doesn't have an answer. There was never an intention to not finishing the stories. Her fondness for collecting is something that is evident from her home. From being in that house so often, from seeing all of her records and the care with which they have obviously been handled, he feels he knows her well.

"I don't know, maybe."

She stares directly at him and closes the book in her lap. Nervous heat bathes his entire body. Her face is cemented doubt. She leans in his direction and whispers loudly as if she's pretending to tell him a secret that everyone knows. She exaggerates the forming of each word with her mouth.

"You should finish reading them."

Her eyes widen and relax as she states her mocking suggestion. Her mouth settles into a self-satisfied grin.

"Eh, where would I find the time?" he manages to joke as his eyes dart around the room and his shoulders mockingly shrug.

She pushes her body back into the smooth, broken-down leather and laughs. Her eyes stay fixed on him as she rests the book in her lap and opens it again. Her left hand reaches up to support her rigid jawline. Her bottom teeth move to the right making room to chew the glowing polished nail of her index finger. He feels her trying to figure him out, and he wonders how soon it will be before she gathers that there is little beyond the apparent to figure. His embarrassment continues to build.

"And what were you reading when I walked in?"

He holds up the flimsy spine paperback that he forgot he had in his hand. She leans in and squints to see the distressed cover.

"Ah, Sartre! How apropos?" she announces in a stuffy British accent.

Her entire body sways to exaggerate her rolling eyes. She continues to laugh. He assumes that at this point, she is only amused with herself. It seems to him that she would probably be laughing at something even if he wasn't there and that makes her likable.

"What? You don't like Sartre?" he lets the rhetorical question sigh out of his mouth as it seems clear to him that she does not.

Her entire body stops and straightens into sarcastic seriousness.

"Sartre's fine, but you can't dance to it."

She releases her earnest expression into laughter once

47

again. This time the chuckle gives way to a snort.

"HAHA! I'm sorry."

Her laughter peaks and holds out into diminishing staccato breaths until it is finally exhausted. Her body falls back into the couch again.

"And will you finish this one?"

She nods in the direction of the book in his hands.

"What, this one?"

He points at the book.

"Oh yeah, for sure! I'll definitely finish this one."

They both grin and quickly look back away from each other. He uncomfortably busies his attention with anything else.

"You should definitely finish that one," she mumbles into the book in her lap.

"I've got no expectations to pass through here again."

The echoes of sleepy, drunken, bar-room piano notes clink together with the empty glasses being cleared after last call. As the song fades away into a hollow vinyl carbonated fizz, he feels as though he has missed out on some incredible inside joke.

.   .   .

At the end of the day, damn how I wish that cliché phrase was even a possibility, it is just less complicated and agonizing to wrap yourself in the ease and comfort of things you know well, but if that solace is all-consuming, if your entire being relies on or is just constant consoling, can that really be life? How long does a person need to be consoled by the familiar until feeling better? Maybe no one feels "good," maybe that's okay. Yes, the world got pretty shitty. Yes, it was pretty fucking miserable, but there are lessons in letting it affect you. There are truly disturbing, painful emotions that you need to feel to be part of the collective consciousness, part of humanity.

Now, it is possible that this concept of needing to experience and see the worst of life to be able to appreciate the entirety of it may just be passed generation to generation like a completely antiquated old wives tale with not even a touch of truth to it. I am not so convinced of my ideals that I cannot fathom that those thoughts may have been instilled to keep everyone from believing that life could be exclusively wonderful. However, I do know that I did not feel whole or even close to resembling something that was once whole before I decided to stay here, and even though the difference is negligible, there is still a difference.

I do know that our new friend must feel something close to

the way I was feeling. It is impossible for me to ignore the fact that all the beautiful and terrible shit that has ever happened made us exactly what we are. Forgetting the past is the worst thing a man can do, except for living in it.

Our new friend hides her unrest better than we do. It would be nearly undetectable except that when she holds her toothy smile a little too long while waiting for a slow response from me, I start to notice her convincing facade begin to crack as the corners of her mouth turn down just slightly. It changes her expression if you are looking hard enough, to an almost stoically hidden disgust. I wonder if she can feel it, if her blushed cheeks get tired and heavy, if the statued sour clench cramps her jaw. I'm sure it would be impossible to notice with any perceivable distraction at all, but I was fixated. It's motherly, not forcing others to deal with your own anguish. We don't have it in us. Women have this selfless care, intrinsically. They are stronger than we are. Their burdens give them something we will never understand or realize, a beguilement we cannot escape.

Joseph D. Newcomer

•　　　•　　　•

5. The Walk

She slams the book closed and tosses it to the seat next to her. Her hands grip the couch cushion and pull her body up to perch on the edge. The noise startles him even though he has not stopped staring at her. He flinches and tries to look away, but her direct eye contact brings his stare right back to her. She leans into the stare and once more shows her toothy wicked grin.

She whispers as loudly as she can, "Let's get shitty!"

The excitement in this idea echoed his feelings from what seems like, and in all fairness may have been, lifetimes ago. He cannot recall the last time he thought of this as a remotely entertaining endeavor. It was just something that happened when it did and with no anticipation or enthusiasm, and after which, there was no regret. Now, with her invite, he is possessed with the notion of the act. He can taste the sickly sweet alcohol on his breath. He can feel the heat of embarrassment settling over his loosened inhibitions. He tries to match the volume of her pretend whisper.

"Yes!"

Surprise in his voice is entirely foreign to him, he never had anyone tell him or know what he wanted to do before he even knew what he wanted to do himself. Simple and complete agreement is the only reaction that his mouth will allow him to give. While standing up, he reaches into the breast pocket of his jacket and pulls out a small silver paper clip. He slides the paper clip onto the pages held open by his finger, allows the book to close around the thin metal, and places the book on the desk beside him. He adjusts his jacket and walks toward the door. She stays clutched to the edge of the couch until he stops at the handrail of the ramp and turns to notice that she hasn't moved.

"Well?" he questions her as he raises his hands and allows them to slap back to his sides.

Her mouth hinges open in unison with her widening eyes. She lets out a tiny shriek of joy, the insignificant volume of which is in complete contrast to the absolute exhilaration of her facial expression and kicking legs. She springs off of the couch and shuffles to him as he continues up the ramp to the door.

Sharp guitars bend in and out of tune over a hissing

marching-band snare drum. A bass thumps up and down scales with the same barroom piano as before, only this time the chords are executed in hurried staccato and not allowed to fully resonate. This time the pace seems ever-quickening, impatiently pushing them through the door. The tone and time of the song flash him a vague, childhood memory of impatiently and ferociously cranking a jack-in-the-box.

"There's a tramp sittin' on my doorstep tryin' to waste his time. With his methylated sandwich, he's a walking clothesline."

He props the door with his foot and allows her past while he bends down to pick up the orange extension cords where they connect, just inside of the building. He pulls the male from the female end of the joined cords and drops them on each side of the doorway. The lyrics quickly drown into a distorted grinding stop.

"And here comes the bishop's daughter on the other side. She looks a trifle jealous. She's been an outcast all her l... i... f... ... e."

He hits the kill switch on the generator. The motor sputters and leaves silence to immediately gather around them. He feels the fast quiet begging for anything to end it, but he is out of practice at idle chit chat and really any type of conversation.

"It really is a perfect day."

She must feel it too, he thinks as she breaks the muted

hush.

"And look at this neighborhood…" she says.

She looks out over the street from the corner of the sidewalk and turns back to him. He approaches her, gestures down the street, and they begin to walk together.

"I mean, it was definitely not like this the last time I saw it. Well, from what I remember."

She points at an antique store window with an elegant display of vintage movie posters, "I mean, where did that come from?"

"These stores were filled with junk. They didn't even bother making displays. It was just a straight, clear shot through the window into broken-down, half-stuffed, stained dolls and dusty, floor-model televisions that didn't look like they ever worked. The whole street was littered with storefronts like that. They were using the word "antique" pretty loosely. It was just old trash that no one wanted. It didn't matter though, because no one was living here anyway and that was way before the Pause." He tries to finish his answer but is sidetracked with the memory of how annoyed he was when he initially saw the run-down neighborhood.

"The PAUSE?" she laughs, "I like that. So, what happened?"

"Well, most of the stores are still filled with junk, but I couldn't bear to see this place like this, so I made the displays, cleaned the windows, and repainted some of the signs. I just wanted to be able to walk down the street."

He struggles through his words. He never imagined this conversation taking place or having to explain this. He knows now that this line of questioning won't end either. He begins formulating answers to the why and how questions that will inevitably follow. Luckily, she is not looking at him. He thanks fate or God or whatever there is to thank for this, as he is sure that his face is contorting in terrifying ways while he tries to concoct reasonable responses. He is desperately trying to act like a normal human being would act from what he remembers of other, normal human beings.

She nods and continues to glance around as they walk. Two blocks pass by in a silence for which he is thankful and satisfied. As he leads her to turn and cross the street, he has nearly forgotten the impending follow-up questions or trying to act like a human being. His anxiety eases at the loss of his inner dialogue.

Halfway across the street, she stops. His relaxed gait takes him a couple of feet before the loss of her presence grasps his neck like a choke collar at the end of a short leash. The overwhelming pull of new concern spins him back to her. She begins a quiet, snorty laugh that increases with every question.

"Why here? Why did you come here, of all the places? Jesus, man! Why the hell would you come here? Did you sweep the streets? Where's all the trash and filth? Couldn't you have found a place that wasn't a shithole already and just stayed there? How long did all of this take? Doesn't it seem a little pointless if no one is ever going to see it? Are you out of your goddamned mind? I fucking love it!"

She is in full-blown hysterics. Her posture is barely held up with her hands clutching her thighs. Her knees awkwardly bend and fold over each other while her toes pigeon inward and her ankles shakingly buckle back and forth over her pointed heels.

While he waits for her to contain herself, he uses the time to recollect his thoughts on how he will explain all of it. When her blushed cheeks even out a little, and she is able to stand without holding onto her legs, he begins to calmly explain.

"I grew up here. When I was a kid, I had a hard time sleeping. We used to go to the planetarium on school field trips and every time, without fail I would fall asleep. Later in life, whenever I had a hard time sleeping I would imagine myself in that planetarium, leaning back, looking up, completely alone. It relaxes me."

She continues to stare at him as though his reasons could never match the absurdity of his choice. Her belly intermittently hiccups with small bits of laughter while he speaks. Her hand is affixed to her pushed-out hip again. He can feel her posture begging for a better explanation.

"The older I got and the further removed I became from this place, the more I felt it pulling me back. Once I got here, I saw how shitty it had become. I still wanted to stay, so I made it look livable. Maybe I just wanted that feeling back, that feeling of falling asleep in that huge room, that empty half-asleep carelessness. But you can't get it back. You can only just barely remember it. How long did it take? That is a tough question. I've been here cleaning and sorting and changing things since a little after it stopped. At this point, I can only tell you with any sort of certainty, that it has been more than three hundred years in any sort of traditional sense. That was when I lost track."

She begins to walk again. He watches as she continues past him. She nods, and he feels as though his plight has been satisfactory. He takes a few steps behind her. She stops abruptly again and turns to him. He scuffs his heels to a stop behind her.

"Wait, why did you lose track?"

"I don't know, I guess I just stopped paying attention on accident."

"You're totally full of shit."

She turns back and continues to walk.

"Wait, no, I'm not lying."

He races to catch up to her.

"No, it's fine, man. I love a good liar. It's almost as nice to be around a good liar as it is difficult to be around some asshole who feels an incessant need to be honest all the time. I'll take a big ol' liar every time, thank you very much."

She speaks without turning back to him while she points her finger straight up in the air as if she is ordering from an imaginary restaurant server. As he catches up to her, she turns her head toward him.

"You do know that there are planetariums in other places, right?" she asks.

He shrugs his shoulders. He actually hadn't thought of that. She laughs, shakes her head, and continues walking.

.   .   .

I can see why. I can empathize with the same needs. We are the same creatures of comfort and habit. That is why I chose to come back here, to where I/we grew up. She asked me why I chose this place. I told her about the draw I felt, the need for rest that made us imagine that fake star-filled dome nearly every night. You know exactly what I mean. That longing you feel now will grow, don't resist it. You should see this place again before it looks like it did when I came back. I have made it as pleasant as I have had the energy to, but it is still not the same. It can't be. It shouldn't be.

I can't tell you how relieved I was that she only asked me, "Why here?" "Why now?" or "Why stay in the Pause?" would have been something I may not have had the stomach with which to respond. Maybe it didn't occur to her to ask. Maybe she already knew. Maybe she is so entirely wrapped in the inevitability of the reality she has created for herself that she no longer believes "when we are" is even relevant. Maybe I'm just projecting. Sometimes it is best to allow certain subjects the silence they deserve. It's an old, comfortable, unhealthy, mutually-abusive relationship we have with existence. We can't stop going back to it and most of us prefer it that way for no good reason.

Most of life is an attempt to construct something to legitimize our instincts. We are just as much a part of this as anyone else. Regardless of our specific choices, we are all the same in that we are merely trying to make it make sense.

Joseph D. Newcomer

●   ●   ●

6. The Drymouth

Sharp, undiffused sunlight cuts through the window leaving an oblong glow with the words "Drymouth Tavern" cut out in stretched italic shadows on the brick-red tile floor of the bar. Reflections from her silver heels dart around the room as she walks through the natural spotlight. Dust kicks up and glows in the beam of light. The luminous particles float into the shadow and disappear. Her heel catches on the broken black grout, and she stumbles. Popcorn trickles out, falling to the floor from the brown wooden bowls she carries. She catches herself, looks up at him, smiles, rights herself, and continues to the stool next to him at the bar.

"You're sure this is still good?" she asks as she slides onto the worn-down barstool.

"I never said it was good, but it probably isn't going to kill you. Have you not been here since it stopped?"

"No, I've never been here."

"You live in this town and you've never been to the Drymouth? What was your life about?"

She shrugs her shoulders and delicately places a few pieces of the yellowed popcorn into her mouth. She picks up a sweating, green bottle of beer as her tongue pushes the popcorn into her cheek. She begins speaking before she can finish chewing. Her jaw stays clenched, and she partially covers her mouth with her hand as she speaks.

"It still makes no sense to me, cold beer, the fluorescent lights in the coolers? I mean, does that jukebox still work?"

She pauses to swallow and point.

"I can't get a single light in my house to turn on. It's a damned good thing that it's daylight."

He cannot help but grin at the feigned politeness of her hand over her mouth. It's as if her body is constantly asking for forgiveness for her casual manners. He begins to feel at ease as he turns to look at the jukebox.

"Yeah, I guess if it was on when it stopped, then that's just the way it will always be."

"Well in this particular case..."

She puts the half-full bottle to her lips and tips her head back as far as it seems it can go. He watches the underside of her chin bounce in rhythm with the bubbles going into the bottle until foamy suds fill its neck. She slams the bottle onto the bar and her chin swings back down to its normal position. Her eyes are watery and as wide open as he has seen them. She belches and half-covers her mouth as her face blushes. She smiles and finishes her sentence from behind her hand.

"... that's... fucking... awesome!"

She stands, wipes her mouth, and half-runs, half-slides her heels across the tile to the jukebox hanging just a few feet away on a brick archway. She takes off her heels and drapes them from her fingers over her shoulder while her other hand taps the "next" button on the machine. Her face glows white in the light of the swinging deck of album track listings. She raises her hand and twirls her heels.

Without looking at him, she yells from her belly in an old-timey English accent, "Shots, my good sir!"

This time he is the imaginary waiter. He walks around the corner of the bar and props the service entrance up onto the wall. He steps behind the bar and shuffles a few bottles around in the well.

"What do you like?" he asks.

She glances at him and turns back to the glow.

"Nothing from down there!"

She flips her jukebox shuffle hand in a shooing motion at him, "Turn around! Get the good stuff."

He turns around and grabs an unopened bottle of scotch. He holds it up to her as she walks back to the bar. She shakes her head with the kind of obvious, grimacing disappointment he'd only seen from his parents when he was much younger.

"Really, man?"

Her features wrinkle and gather to the center of her face in disappointed disgust.

He puts the bottle back and turns back to her.

"So, what do you want?"

"HOLY FUCK!"

They are both startled by a new, thunderous, booming voice that overpowers the room. They whip their attention to the man at the center of the bar whose stature matches his roaring tone perfectly.

She rights her body back onto the barstool and looks away from the screaming giant. With her eyes locked back onto her more familiar new friend, her entire body is in a paralyzed clench of laughter and fear.

Her face, eyes, and mouth are all shouting, but all that comes out is an almost silent whispering, "What the fuck?"

He laughs from behind the bar, "Ha, don't worry, that's just Shaffer."

She looks back at the imposing figure as it reaches for a half-collapsed, cellophane-covered, soft-pack of cigarettes on the bar, pulls out a cigarette, and lights it. The flame jumps from the end of the cigarette with a small gray drift of smoke as the Zippo snaps closed. His first draw is long and deep, forcing the man's broad slumped shoulders to fully extend out, away from his body where they stop for a beat. Slowly, his stretched back recedes, relaxing his frame and forcing the inhaled smoke out into the bar. The stale, gray fog races in and out of the beams of light from the window while the cloud steadily grows to fill the room.

Three shot glasses clack onto the bar.

"I know exactly what the big guy is having."

He grabs a bottle of Hornitos Reposado and holds it up to her.

"Tequila?" he raises his eyebrows with the question.

"Oh yeah, I'll have what he's having."

She leans up onto the bar with her elbows and rests her

cheeks on her palms while he picks up the shot glasses with the tips of his fingers and shoves the bottle of liquor under his arm. He grabs three bottles of beer from the cooler and makes his way back around to the patron's side of the bar. When he gets to the waiting girl, he stops and motions for her to walk ahead of him through the cloud of smoke and the large man's shadow to the seat at the bar. The large man is still oblivious to their presence.

As they come closer to the new figure, it blocks the light from the window, and he comes into focus. Still holding the cigarette in his teeth, he washes his face with his hands and rubs his eyes, with his fingertips then with his palms. He gently smacks his own face and scratches at his wiry goatee and the stubble on the soft, fleshy area under his chin. Standing alongside him, watching his waking ritual, they are entirely eclipsed in his shadow. His hearty physique dwarfs them in both height and build, but he is proportioned well and his frame is inviting. He has an oversized, teddy-bear attraction that begs to be hugged.

"He still doesn't even know we're here," he leans to her and whispers while pouring three shots into the glasses on the bar just a few seats down from the smoking man.

"Huh," she hums through her closed teeth and jutted jaw while she nods.

He continues to whisper as to not startle their new company, "I fucking love this guy. He's a riot. I've known him forever. If it were possible to go back with someone, I'd definitely go back with him and relive some of our wilder nights. I've seen him a handful of times since the Pause. I used to come here all the time, in hopes of catching him between his trips. I don't come by as often now though. We used to hang out here a million years ago, when we were kids. We'd shoot the shit and hit on girls, unsuccessfully, most of the time."

He opens the three beers, one by one, with a bottle opener sitting on the bar in front of them and continues his story while he hands her the fresh drink.

"Anyway, when he was back here for a few minutes between trips, if I was lucky enough to catch him, we'd have a couple of beers, and he'd tell me what he was up to. You know, in the past of course. After a while, his visits got shorter and a few beers turned into maybe a shot or a quick drag of a smoke."

"Why?"

She seems genuinely heartbroken at his story.

"Well, at first he would go back and his trips would be pretty short. He would go to some insane time and party until he got bored or died in some whacked out way, like old west barroom shoot-outs, or Woodstock acid trips gone wrong. One time he told me that he was actually eaten by a fucking dinosaur. If he stays long enough to talk, don't bring up the dinosaur. That one still freaks him out, and we will never hear the end of how the feather thing was a load of shit, trust me. At some point, he met a girl. Are you familiar with the movie, *Groundhog Day*?"

"Yes, I love Bill Murray!"

"Of course you do. He's the best. Anyway, Shaf's been Groundhog Daying the shit out of this girl that he fell in love with, and ever since he met her, he can't wait to get back and make her fall in love with him again. It's pretty impressive, too. The last time we spoke he told me the longest he had managed to keep the relationship perfect for her was over three of her years. Can you imagine, dedicating your existence to making one person's life perfect because that's what keeps you satisfied? With all the things that I know and love him for, brash, loud, foul-mouthed, opinionated Shaffer has defied his nature to show this one girl his soft, sweet, gooey, chivalrous center. Ethics aside, it seems like the least pointless of all the trivial pursuits that I can imagine."

"Awe, that is kinda sweet… in a sick, stalkery sort of way," she giggles, "What does he do when he screws it up?"

"Sky's the limit! Hookers, blow, robs banks, whatever gets him back here the fastest while also being the most entertaining."

"Jesus! I love this guy. Am I going to get to meet him?"

"Maybe, he has been here for a while. He must be watching an auto-reload or something."

She reaches out her silver pump and nudges the man's side.

"Shaffer," she whispers.

She follows it up with two more heel nudges and an even louder whisper.

"Shaffer."

The large man is unaffected and continues to stare straight into the mirror behind the bar. What very little is left of his cigarette is now barely clinging to the corner of his mouth and his bottom lip.

"That's not going to work. I have a better idea."

He picks up one of the overflowing shot glasses and hands it to her. He grabs the other two and holds one out, just under the big man's nose. Tequila drips onto the bar. Shaffer's nostrils flare as his left hand reaches for the cashed and barely smoldering cigarette filter. As he pulls the butt out of his mouth, a crazy, cartoon, Cheshire Cat grin overcomes his face. His half-closed eyelids disappear as his eyes pop open, and he belts out his words with his entire body.

"HA, NOW THAT'S WHAT I'M TALKIN' BOUT!"

Shaffer's entire being lights up. He grabs the shot and downs it in one motion. He slams the tiny glass on the bar while his head whips away from the two onlookers. His entire body jerks and the words fly out of his mouth like dust off of a shaken rug.

"GOD... DAMN IT, THAT'S GOOD! AH!"

His eyes clamp closed. He reaches for the glass and slides it back down the bar while belching into his fist, away from his company. At the end of his arm, sprawled out and resting on the bar, he leaves his hand open, clearly signaling for another. They watch him in humored amazement. She leans up to the bar between the two men, grabs the bottle, pours another, and places it into the hulking, outstretched hand. He holds the tiny shot glass gently between his massive thumb and forefinger. He pulls the drink to his body. Just as the tequila is directly in front of him, he taps the bottom of the glass on the bar and simultaneously nods his head. Still, without having acknowledged their presence, he puts the shot to his bottom lip, tips his head back, and empties the glass into his mouth. This time all three of them take their shot at the same time. Shaffer's glass rolls into the palm of his hand. He clenches his fist around the glass and presses it against his chest. His face shakes and quivers with pure pleasure. He spins his barstool and his body to their gawking, grinning faces.

As Shaffer's eyes open, they are directly focused on the bullet spinning next to the girl's head. His face quickly puzzles into widened concern.

"WHAT THE FUCK IS..."

71

The smaller man leans around the girl, frantically shaking his head and making cutting motions with his hand to his neck. He had almost completely forgotten that the bullet even exists. He catches Shaffer's eye before the question is finished. Shaffer's face jumps from worry into a nodding smile of understanding and his voice mellows.

"...UP? What the fuck is up, man? How the hell are ya?"

"I'm doing great, Shaf. Just having a few drinks with a new friend."

The smaller man's relief pours out between his words with his unnecessarily held breath. He isn't sure why it is so important that something so obvious not be pointed out, and he cannot believe how quickly he had blocked out the fact that it was there. He wonders how he had allowed it to become the same sort of ignored, pale flicker that once helped him keep track of "when" he would be, hadn't time given up on them.

Shaffer grabs the open beer off of the bar and points at the jukebox with it.

"Well, why isn't there any music playing? It's happy hour for Christ's sake."

He takes a sip of the beer and slides the bottle back onto the bar. His enormous hand pulls the half-pack of Winston Lights back to him. He pulls out three cigarettes, puts them in his mouth, and lights them all.

"Shaffer, it's always happy hour," the smaller man scoffs.

Shaffer carefully grabs two of the cigarettes, one in each hand, leaving one in the center hanging from his lip. He hands a cigarette to each of them. His voice raises again, belting and distorting out of the sides of his mouth around the lit Winston.

"YOU'RE GODDAMNED RIGHT IT IS!"

The cherry of Shaffer's cigarette flashes with the wind of his breath. Small bits of white ash are blown at the two onlookers.

"I didn't have any cash," she answers through a suppressed laugh.

Shaffer stands and reaches over a cash register across the bar, in front of him. He casually taps a few buttons. The drawer dings and flies open. He pulls a handful of cash back over the top of the drawer and drops it on the bar. With the cigarette still hanging from his mouth, he grabs a crumpled ten-dollar bill and flattens it out between the edge of the bar and the meat of his hand. He slides the bill down the bar to her.

"Hey darlin', here's a sawbuck. Play something nice, nothing from after 2005 unless it's from a band that was good before 1995, okay?"

He holds his finger on top of the bill until she responds.

"OK!"

Her eyes dart to her companion. They grin while she grabs the bill and her beer, jumps down from her stool, does an exaggerated, cartoon about-face, and runs to the jukebox.

Shaffer taps the bar, leans in, and whispers while he glances over at the girl.

"What the fuck is with the...?" he points his finger at his head and makes a quiet gun shooting sound, "I mean, how the hell does that work?"

"I honestly have no idea."

They stare at her as she leans her head on her forearm against the jukebox. Her other hand rests against the keypad. She intermittently taps the buttons to cycle through the selections.

"Well, anyway, it's good to fucking see ya!" Shaffer says, reaching for the tequila and pouring three more shots.

"How's Kate?" the smaller man asks.

"You know, it was going pretty well. Then her sister's new husband says some bullshit about how Pearl Jam never wrote anything decent after *Ten*, and it's a wedding reception, so you know I'm wasted. Anyway, this time I tell him he's an asshole. Long story short, apparently, you can't call your girlfriend's sister's husband an asshole at his wedding reception."

"This time! So this has happened before?"

"Yeah, this is the second time," Shaffer responds between blowing out cigarette smoke and taking a sip of his beer.

"What happened the first time?"

"I called him a fucking asshole."

They both laugh.

Simple, silent-film, piano music fades into the bar. Shaffer ashes his cigarette and cocks his head to the side. His eyebrows raise as his head sinks into his shoulders and his neck disappears. A goofy grin of recognition smears his teeth across his face. His head jumps up, away from his shoulders, and spins to look at the girl at the jukebox.

"BOWIE!" he laughingly shouts to her in a cracking high pitch of surprise as the lyrics begin.

"Wake up you sleepyhead. Put on some clothes shake up your bed."

"GOOD GIRL! I fucking LOVE BOWIE."

Shaffer picks up two of the shots, slides the other to his friend, and dances one over to the girl at the jukebox. They hold their glasses up to their friend at the bar, and they all drink together. Shaffer tosses his shot glass over his shoulder. He grabs the girl's right hand with his right hand, pulling her away from the jukebox and into a stumbling spin which lands her face thumping into the pillow of his broad chest. Paralyzed with laughter, she is completely and voluntarily under the large man's control. He pushes her into his body and lifts her slightly, effortlessly. He extends her arm with his hand grasped around hers and swings her around in the wide expanse of the brick archway, back and forth over its threshold.

The man at the bar watches her naked toes as they extend to find any sort of footing, but they can just barely graze the floor. Shaffer sings in a beautiful, rich, striking baritone overpowering the volume of the jukebox. His voice is octaves lower than the song, but he is in perfect harmony with the key. As the classic refrain approaches, his head tilts back to face the ceiling, his eyes clench closed, and she begins to sing with him. His words explode with the start of the driving bass line of the chorus. His resonant voice blasts through the bar, echoing off of the ceiling and nearly drowning out her high-pitched harmony completely. As he dances her around the floor, she is even more muffled by his chest and her own laughter.

"OH! YOU PRETTY THINGS, DON'T CHA KNOW YOU'RE DRIVIN' YOUR MAMAS AND PAPAS INSANE?"

The smaller man continues to quietly watch the large man and the dead girl while the nearly transparent visions of his memories with Shaffer in the bar play over the entire scene. He smiles as the couple dances through the trace apparitions his mind is projecting around the room.

.　　　.　　　.

It is easier than I can explain to get so involved with your current situation that you allow yourself to forget the person you were before whatever it is that is happening right now, happened. That is, until nothing happens to you for so long that you are able to think about all the different people you used to be, the strong-willed person who was able to walk away from anyone in any situation that wasn't one hundred percent in line with his self-determined code of existence, the forgiving person who allowed people back into his good graces, the naive kid that designed hopeful ideals just to have them changed or forfeited when it suited who life decided he was later.

It's important to keep people in your life, people who have known you forever, people who have known all the different people you have been. They know how far you've come. They can tell you when you've gone too far. Do whatever you can to keep them around for as long as you can. If your timeline has a course similar to this one, you'll be grateful for even the most infinitesimal amount of their company.

.   .   .

Shaffer falls back into his chair. His blushed face glistens with the mist of the first sign of sweat.

"Goddamn!" he exclaims through his teeth as they cradle a new cigarette.

The Zippo clinks open and sparks flash next to his thumb. Tiny beads of perspiration reflect the orange glow and brighten his face. The lighter fluid and smoke hang around the three of them giving a palpable, sweet, toxic flavor to the air.

"Gotta catch my breath here, darlin'."

Shaffer takes a long drink from his bottle.

"How the fuck am I out of breath and all fucking sweaty?"

He wipes his brow and looks at his hand.

"I mean, what the fuck?"

He holds his wet hand out to his small friend.

"Look at this shit! Isn't fucking time stopped? I mean, is it just me?"

"Shaffer, man, it's great to see you. I feel like it's been way too long."

"Dude, I see you all the time! Well, not you, now you, but you. Young you and I and young me hang out in this bar all the time. We were such assholes! In the best way possible, of course," Shaffer responds while he smokes between unnecessary labored breaths.

"Well, I'm happy to hear that me, not me is having a good time and hanging out with you and young you. I honestly don't think I can even imagine that."

"What are you saying? It's AWESOME! Did you hear me mention there are two of me? You're having a GREAT fucking time."

As the smaller man laughs, he tries to bury the urge growing in the base of his skull, the urge begging him to mourn for his friend's imminent departure. He begins to fight missing this moment before Shaffer can finish his sentence. While he has always found Shaffer's animated, widening eyes and intermittent shouting to be incredibly hilarious, he knows there is a great depth of character there as well. He regrets there will most likely be no time for meaningful conversation of any kind, but the laughs are a welcomed relief for as long as they can overshadow the burden of his knowing, at some point, Shaffer will forget that this ever happened, that they ever knew each other. Eventually, Shaffer will forget everything and that depth of character which was once so obvious will be gone along with the memories that dug it into his psyche.

He glances over to the girl to make sure she is still as entertained by Shaffer as he and Shaffer are. He sees the same overjoyed look of bewilderment on the girl's face as he feels on his own. He watches her return to the jukebox. His and Shaffer's laughs fade to a whimper while the girl resumes making song selections.

Steady, delicate, deliberate piano chords accent weary swells of violin and slowly bowed strings. The drawn-out notes arch over smoldering bassy embers of a rumbling cello as they ease their way through the bar.

"Jesus, dude! Where did you find her?" Shaffer asks.

The grinding voice of a giant, rusted-hinge door scrapes through the solemn tones with an ancient unmistakable, sharp, howling timbre of wisdom and soul. The familiarity of the voice immediately makes the smaller man smile and nod. As he looks at Shaffer, he sees the same satisfied grin.

"I kept the right ones out, and let the wrong ones in."

Shaffer softly closes his eyes and, in unison with the lyrics, he dramatically sings, "HAD AN ANGEL OF MERCY TO SEE ME THROUGH ALL MY SINS."

He opens his eyes and shakes his head.

"FUCK, man! It's tough to leave when Aerosmith is playing, but I have to get back. There are people that don't even know they're missing me back there and it just wouldn't be fair to them, you know?"

"For sure! You need to go save them from their empty, vapid lives. It must be so difficult for them to harbor such a bottomless pit in their being with no idea of why it's even there. I can't even imagine what any of us did before there were two of you."

Shaffer takes another shot.

"It's just a goddamned shame there aren't three of me. A GODDAMNED SHAME, I TELL YOU!"

The shot glass and his hand smack against the bar, punctuating the end of his sentence. Both men chuckle as they hug and smack each other on the back. As the girl approaches them, the two men separate. Shaffer reaches for the girl's hand, pulls it to him, and gently kisses the back of it.

"You dance like a drunken angel and your taste in music is exquisite. The pleasure was all mine."

She smiles as he sits and turns back to the bar. He shouts again with the beginning of the end of the chorus.

"WHOA, IT'S AMAZING!"

He disappears.

"And I'm saying a prayer for the desperate hearts tonight."

The girl's face is lit up with shock. She laughs and points to Shaffer's empty seat.

"Now THAT, is an EXIT! WOW!"

.   .   .

It can be difficult to not hate people for their decisions and for how their decisions, ultimately, affect your own life. Even though I understand the logic and reason, even though it makes me appreciate that she might share my ideals about how meaningless life is becoming, has become, I still struggle to not judge the dead girl for trying to kill herself. I try not to feel disappointed in Shaffer for continuing to knowingly lose his memories and, eventually, his entire original being on entertaining himself with pretend lives. I also cannot stand that this judgment and disappointment even enters my thoughts, it gives me a bitter loathsome feeling about my own narcissism. Only semantics separate our concepts of what is real and important. Calling his lives "pretend" because of my own hang-ups is only, truly, a deflection.

What I honestly feel is an addition to my compounding loss. I will miss my friend. I will always wonder who the dead girl was before she pulled the trigger. These are my burdens, not theirs. These selfish notions are not useful thoughts by which to base their character. You can't decide how other people should feel and then be disappointed in them for not feeling the way you decided they should, but we all do it. Other people are not you, you shouldn't want them to be, it's not possible, and you wouldn't like them if they were.

While it would be easy to write them off for their choices simply because I disagree with them, the harder thing to do is to understand, to allow myself to empathize with a choice when I don't believe I would have made it. What you'll learn after all of this lack of time and seeing people that you love and respect, intelligent people, people you know to be reasonable and decent, as they make choices that you can't believe or accept, is that people just want to belong. People want to belong somewhere--school, a career, a circle of friends, an actual physical location, with a specific person. When that want isn't satisfied by something most people would consider normal, that want can easily allow itself to be satisfied by something that may even be detrimental to the person it drives--drugs, cults, the past, the Pause. Time stopping hasn't taken that want from us yet, but I worry that being able to live in the past, that being able to search all of time to find where we feel we belong has falsely convinced us that our want is being satisfied. I remember feeling that way, satisfied, and most times I wish I still did.

My want to belong wishes the people I care about felt the same way as I do now, so we could share in that commonality together, here in the Pause. The best parts of me hope they are just able to go on with their lives forever, feeling satisfied regardless of why or how, without the burden of my ideals, however justified or unjustified or wrong or right they may be. I know that you'll stand on and hold firmly to your belief that (what you consider to be) the poor decisions of others, come from weakness, but it is not weakness. The ability to allow yourself to believe in something that may only exist to take advantage of that ability is the same thing that allows you to care about anything. I can't fault Shaffer for allowing himself to feel satisfied and happy, even if I don't think that it's real. This ability we have to convince ourselves that the things we consider to be "right" are absolutely correct is the strongest innate ability that we possess. It is real to him. It is as real to him as my belief, that it is not, is to me. The way he feels is real. His emotions are definitely real, and they seem a hell of a lot more enjoyable than mine. I mean, who the fuck am I? Aren't we all just guessing?

I also don't blame her, as I've already said. If a person doesn't find someone, some where, some thing, or some time to be a part of or to belong to, if a person doesn't feel like they have the option or ability to try to any longer, it doesn't mean that want goes away. They must feel that they are only left with two options to end that emptiness, either destroy the world around them or take themselves out of it. While it kills me to think anyone would feel that way, how I feel about it doesn't make it any less a reality for people that do. We learn to accept and love our prisons, but only because they are our own. It is impossible to fully understand anyone else, but if you can, at the very least, try to validate how they came to their prison before you choose to disregard their entire being, you'll learn a greater deal from them than you would have otherwise. If it is ever possible to give someone a reason to feel as though they are a part of, or that they do belong to someone, some thing, some where, some time, give it to them, and maybe you'll allow their want to be satisfied in a way that saves you both.

.   .   .

"I feel drunk. Can we actually even get drunk, or is it just in our heads?" she asks cheek resting on her freckled hand, flat on the bar top.

She twists her bottle in front of her face with her fingers, allowing the bottom to roll and rumble like a spinning coin coming to a stop on the bar while the last sips of beer inside stay parallel to the counter.

Without the distraction of the large man's volume and spectacle of his presence, the room feels dead to the smaller man. He sees the pleasant glow of amusement draining off of her, and he questions his decision to bring her here.

"You know, I'm not sure. If I'm not drunk, I guess I'm easily convinced because I feel shit faced."

Looking into her bottle, she smiles at his response.

"You do seem pretty gullible," she says, glancing back at him.

"How sweet of you to say!"

He laughs and finishes his beer.

.   .   .

Knowing any level of excitement multiplies the weight of this endless restlessness once that excitement is gone. In the Pause, sometimes it's better to be as still as possible to allow yourself to lose the expectation of this reality being anything more than it is capable of being. This depth of boredom is the greatest rival of happiness, and we may never escape it now knowing what life is like without the existence of boredom, without being perfectly and constantly entertained. We are damned by amazement and awe, no longer inspired by it.

.   .   .

"I think I get it. I was thinking about your living situation and I think I understand," her voice slurs, but only very slightly.

Her elbow presses against the bar top and her hand holds the full weight of her leaning head. With each of her boozy, exaggerated facial movements, her loose red curls extend and recoil, dancing around her delicate, milk forearm. Her eyes are relaxed. Each blink is slower, softer, and easier than the one before.

"Well, as long as I have your blessing, I guess I feel much better about my life choices."

His response entertains her more than he imagined it might. Her late and unsolicited approval entertains him more than it should have. They laugh loudly enough and long enough to make him uncomfortable. His laughter subsides into a forced breath.

"Where would you move? Where would you like to be if you could, and you can, mind you, live anywhere? I'm guessing, not a planetarium, right?" he asks.

"HA! No, a planetarium is fine. It's not what I'd pick, but it's not void of a certain poetic elegance. I can dig it. But yeah, it probably wouldn't be my first choice."

"Okay, so what would be?" he asks again.

Her face sobers and it seems she is actually, truly considering the question.

"Anywhere, huh?"

She bites the corner of her bottom lip as her eyes glance up and to her left, away from the conversation. She smirks, and her eyes quickly return to his.

"Disneyland!"

She bursts into laughter. Her middle finger rests on the tip of her nose while her hand poorly masks her mouth from him. He guesses to himself as to why she would try to cover her smile, why she would attempt to hide her obvious joy, what it was or who it was that instilled a reason in her to feel embarrassed by anything about her uncontrollable expressions of overwhelmed elation. Was it learned or was it another of our countless ingrained embarrassments, so impossible to pinpoint an origin for that they seem innate? He also cannot begin to imagine what made her answer so uproariously funny, nor can he understand why he is laughing again, as well.

She clears her throat to halt her laughing.

"But seriously, seriously…"

She clears her throat once more, tucks her hair behind her ears, and rests her chin on her palm.

"Seriously, I don't know. Graceland, maybe, or maybe somewhere by the ocean with a pier and a roller coaster-like Santa Monica or Atlantic City."

"I have the universe in my living room and you make fun of me, but you would have been completely alright with Coney Island? Okay! I get it!" he mocks her.

He walks around the bar to get them another round. She continues to talk, but he can barely hear her as he walks away. At this point, he thinks she is really only thinking aloud.

"Yeah, roller coasters and cotton candy and the beach. Oh, my God! I love the beach."

He hands her a beer from behind the bar.

"Sure, Coney Island, why the hell not?"

He jokes, but he can see the idea breathing life into her. Her wants are becoming his. He wishes he could satisfy each of them.

"So we know what type of area you would choose, but

where would you sleep, on the Ferris wheel? What kind of house would you have, a normal beach bungalow, a penthouse overlooking the water, a rickety carnie trailer?"

She looks off into the back corner of the bar where she found her initial idea. Her hair chases her excited, wide-eyed face back around to him.

"No, a theater. The classic kind with bright round light bulbs everywhere and red velvet with gold trim everything. It smells like stale popcorn and it always feels like something exciting is about to happen."

He can see on her satisfied face that she is actually there in her mind.

•　　　•　　　•

7. The Way It Was

If we didn't know what it was that was keeping this world haphazardly stumbling along through time, then our best guess was faith or luck. I cannot figure which of those things is more miraculous. I'm not certain I believe one or the other, or either for that matter. Maybe it is the sum of everything we do and everything that happens because of what we do, which kept us all trudging through existence.

We were creating and changing and evolving, not only in our physical nature, but in our ideas and understandings of what we were and why we were here. Even if our concepts were weak or wrong or even if they were on a path which would have never been remotely enlightening, even if, despite the belief that we were aspiring to some greater sophistication, we were only actually in an entropic free fall, we were still doing something and that something had an effect. When that effect ceased, so did any hope of anything after it being any different from what existed at that exact moment.

Maybe time stopped for the same reason I stopped going back. Maybe it couldn't stand not having the ability to create anything, regardless of how subtle or insignificant. Maybe time stopped so that subtle, insignificant changes would mean everything.

.   .   .

She leans back into the seat, forcing the backrest into a reclining position. Her high heels clack onto the floor. Her toes curl around the top edge of the back of the chair in front of them. A dim blue glow traces the lines of her face and body. There is just enough light for him to make out her expressions, but he feels it is somehow dark enough for him to look directly at her without it being uncomfortable. From a loosely rolled joint, the slow red-orange burn of campfire light warms over her face and eclipses everything else into blackness as she draws in and holds her breath. The ember and her face fade quickly back to the cool glow of the planetarium. The smoldering light of the joint floats closer to him, and he reaches out to it. Fog and musk snake through the dim air.

He takes a drag and watches the rolling reflection of the star-washed ceiling in her eye while she begins to speak over the giant, empty room's heavy weighted hum.

"If you could end this, would you? If it meant it was completely over, no going back, would you want it to stop if it meant time would start again?"

"Of course I would!" he responds without thinking.

This has been his prevailing wish since even before he stopped going back. It is a gut reaction that he would want time to continue. Immediately, he regrets not thinking about it first, not reconsidering how he feels before he spoke. Now, since he met her, he is no longer so certain. She comes back too quickly for him to change his answer.

"Really? What if it meant nothing would really change? People would go back to being the same shits they were before the Pause, and Nostalgia, Inc., and time travel? If it meant all the worst things about them would just come back and everyone would go right back to idolizing their own torture, just incessantly feeding the machine? Now, even though you are beyond the trivial crush of it all, you would want to go back?"

A cruel accusing sneer pushes her lip up over her teeth. Her eyebrows distort her forehead into disbelief, but her brow line relaxes quickly into disappointment as she continues, "Somehow, by some freak chance you escape the sad, seemingly inevitable fate of humanity and all of its horrors and you just want it to go right back to the way it was?"

"Well, now I'm not so sure! You don't want time to move again?"

"I'm not saying that I don't."

She pauses to take another hit of the joint.

"I just don't understand why you would. Everyone used to worry about how it would all end. Now that there is no imaginable end in sight, you want to go back to worrying about how it will all end again. It's pretty funny."

She sits up and slides to the edge of her seat to speak directly at him.

"Fate doesn't have to be an end. Sometimes, the worst fate is one which has no end."

Her eyebrow jumps and she explodes into laughter. He laughs with her again, and again he is unsure why he is laughing. He is more confused than entertained but entertained nonetheless.

.　　.　　.

The way things were. I guess it's tough to imagine a reason why anyone would want that again. Back then, we at least had a puncher's chance. All we had to do was get people to be more compassionate, which is, apparently, an even greater feat than stopping time. IEODs did seem to stop people from hating each other for a time and it did seem to make things better, but only because once people had it, we stopped caring about our own agendas, our false understanding of the human condition, and our each and every socioeconomic and political issue. It wasn't that we were taking time to understand people we didn't agree with or that we accepted that our differences were what made life and ourselves valuable. We were incapable of allowing ourselves to be, in any way, satisfied with life in general. We all didn't reach some reasonable agreement based on some sort of miraculous common ground compromise. No, instead we were just so enamored with a new way to block out all the negativity that we stopped giving a fuck. We felt we would never have to compromise about anything that would actually change the world or challenge anything in it ever again. Back then, the solutions were difficult, not impossible, but nothing was ever solved, and we just went right on being the horrible people we are, even if we were only doing it silently in our own minds.

Sometimes, I think that I wish we would all just learn our lesson, get what's coming to us, finally reap what we've so poorly sown. But always, the very next thought is that I don't really know

96

if I could wish that kind of hard truth or understanding on anyone, including you, including myself.

I suppose our true nature just lies dormant with time, our vastly sprawling unresolved issues, and all of our unrealized potential. The dead girl could very well be right, if time ever does start, maybe we would have to face it all over again. Maybe all of our ignorance and hatred are just waiting there for us. Humankind didn't invent tragedy or death or suffering, but we sure as hell made great strides in perfecting it. I don't know if all of that can ever just go away.

Our most significant failure before what might have been our final, was not realizing how similar we were. We imagined ourselves as unique from one another in our rebellious notions or our conformist ideals. We celebrated our disconnection and our discontent, and we allowed ourselves to be weakened by the inner conflict of our need for individuality and our need to feel connected. We subscribed to and idolized things and people that purposefully took advantage of our weaknesses and confused our beliefs. It's just as easy to control the actions of rebellious people as it is to control the actions of conformists, especially if what you want is for nothing to happen, especially if your goal is to halt progress and keep things exactly as they are.

Once we were able to see, or once we were convinced that even rebellion was truly conformity, both words lost their meanings and it didn't matter anymore if it was the truth or a lie, there wasn't a difference. What we created, or what we were seduced into creating, was an eternal conflict without any hope for resolution.

We championed these ideas and people and even inanimate luxuries, and we felt they represented us, but they were corrupted. Nothing represented us any longer. We were placated and patronized by figures that merely feigned to be our voice or uphold our best interests while they pushed antiquated ideologies, ideologies that had been so convoluted over time that their original intents were not even as much as a whisper in their then-current doctrines. The people we had been taught all of our lives to respect and honor exploited our trust and admiration only to further their own personal status. They did such an incredible job that they may have even convinced themselves that their actions were altruistic.

We were all snared by the worst kind of weapons, steeped in the guise of tradition. The things we enjoyed were fashioned into tools with which to gather a better understanding of our nature, solely in order to more effectively manipulate us. This is how we were living long before IEODs were even a thought. It is completely understandable as to how we were wholly consumed, how quickly we could fall in love with something that could so easily take all of that away.

.   .   .

As it rises, her lithe figure sways between the rows of seats. The ember floats toward him again. It draws a fading luminous line behind itself through the darkness. Her hand softly and cautiously lingers against his until he has full control of the joint. Her hands decidedly clasp to her hips while she surveys the room. She scans the dark recesses as if she has just finished a task and is giving it one last look-over.

Looking up at her from his seat, she is a towering shadowed monument, floating against a backdrop of celestial lights. He closes one eye as his vision begins to blur and double. She looks back at him and smiles again.

"Well, I guess it's getting late," the blurry vision of her jokes.

He nods his head, looks at his bare wrist to continue her joke.

"Yeah, you're right. I mean, would you look at the time!"

She awkwardly swings her arms and points to his crossed legs hanging over the seat in front of him. He jumps to stand and allow her through the aisle.

"I'm just going to…"

He interrupts her, "Do you want me to walk you home?"

He is pleased with his immediate reaction coming this time without hesitation. He thinks that maybe his connection to the common pleasantries of human interaction isn't entirely lost. It is not just a pleasantry though, while there is nothing that could be construed as dangerous between the planetarium and her house, he is still concerned with her well-being for reasons he can't fully bring himself to understand.

Squeezing between him and the seat in front of him, she carefully slides past him. She moves cautiously, not allowing her body to brush against his.

"No, you stay."

She walks past the few seats to the end of the aisle and turns back to him.

"I am way too fucked up to continue to hear myself talk. Besides, I don't want to reveal all of my secrets. After all, I'm a lady."

She flutters her eyelashes and delicately places the fingertips of her right hand to the center of her chest as she mockingly curtsies.

"And I'm sure you have so many things to half-read and half-do."

She grins and raises her eyebrows. They both smile. She points to the bright outline of daylight shining through the crack around the door.

"I'll just let myself out."

She stops at the desk in the center of the room and turns on the lamp. She kneels down to the floor next to the desk where his backpack sits on top of the facedown typed pages in a wooden tray. He hears the bag unzip.

"I'm going to take some of this pot with me," she yells back to him.

"Sure!" he answers to what he knows was clearly not a question.

Her hand shuffles in the bag for a moment. She stands up, shoves her hand into the front pocket of her jeans, and pulls her Clash tee shirt down to cover her pocket.

He laughs, "You know, no one is here to see that? It's not like you need to hide it."

"Ah, yeah. I guess you're right."

Her voice sounds shaky and embarrassed. He nods and waves as she quickly looks back at him. She turns away, hurries up the ramp, and leaves. He waits while she walks through the door. As the door closes, he stands and stumbles to the center of the room, turns off the projector, and slides the house lights up just enough to see his home. He sits at the desk and begins slowly pecking at the keyboard of the typewriter.

.   .   .

I've spent centuries thinking about how much better it would be if things could go back to the way they used to be. I told you, I'm just as guilty of dragging the past with me as anyone. We are all out of sync with the way life tries to move us. We buck and pull back on something greater than we could ever hope to control. This is the result. We no longer have to accept where life has taken us, but in turn, we have forfeited our ability to move forward. You cannot go backward and continue to move forward, you cannot stand still and expect to benefit from either direction.

Until now, I have never had to consider anything that might happen if time started again as a consequence. Even in my most optimistic belief, there is only a slight possibility that time will ever continue. We want it for different reasons. I want what life used to be, or at least I think that I thought I did. She seems even more conflicted, neither wanting to stay here nor move forward, and I can only guess by the bullet that she was finished going back or once she realized that was impossible, she aimed for a direction which was none of the given options.

If the clock ticks, she will be gone, that is clearly what she wanted, but I don't think or cannot believe that is all that she wants. I do know she has given me a new reservation about my hope for time to resume. There must be something more that I cannot see driving her, something that she'd like to forget, some sort of hope that she is hiding, that she probably wishes she didn't have, that she had to have thought was gone before she decided to pull the trigger. Now, that "something" seems to linger around her. I guess it could just be what I want or the only way I can allow myself to justify it.

It may also just be the decided and stubborn end that follows every move of her temple. Still, she is less inhibited than we are, less held back by the burden of ideals. She is freer than we can ever understand, more open than we are able to be. We all hide something because we assume the truth is something no one would believe, something we would prefer not to believe ourselves or about ourselves and that is the greatest lie with which humanity has ever convinced itself--our greatest distraction from being truly and entirely satisfied, but this is not the case for her. She cannot base her wants on the same simple notions as the living, and she is not distracted by the entitlement of an ability which allows us to choose when and who we want to be. We are spoiled by the fact that only our opinions matter to us now. Her life is confined to this moment and even this moment is already over for her.

She never really answered if she wants time to continue. It seems she is being punished either way. The choices seem equal to her and now, with her here, I wonder which is the lesser of these two muted hypothetical evils. Knowing my opinion makes no difference is my only escape from this thought. The only resolution I can come away with is that it's still good to feel any way about anything, to consider even the most improbable of circumstances and to be affected by belief, however wavering or uncertain. This is something she has pulled back to my surface, this what would you do if...? I'd given up on considering the impossible particular scenario of my future until she was here, even though it happening is no more likely now than it was before her. I do remember a time when what would happen next was a constant consideration.

Damn, when did we stop being obsessed with the future? Probably right before we started obsessing about a time in the past when we used to be obsessed with the future. Again, we are all guilty. Maybe right now, while fate isn't an end, I can give her something to feel anything about, something that I've already done and has been waiting for her since before she had to think about it. Maybe I can give her a reason to feel as though she belongs here, to this place, that she's not just stuck in this endless moment.

.   .   .

He flips the projector switch and slowly pulls the house lights down until only the stars guide his way to the couch. The worn leather huffs and groans as he rolls his body out, onto the seats. He imagines that even death is less still than the air around him. His eyes close and he concentrates on his habitual breathing. The nearly transparent static blur of his IEOD plays against the back of his eyelids. He is almost surprised to see that the programming is still running at all.

"One hundred percent transparency," he says aloud, knowing he only needs to think it.

The subtle illumination of the graying haze vanishes and perfect, pure, black emptiness is all that is left. The pristine darkness envelops him. He forces his eyes open to escape the feeling that he has been blinded to even his own thoughts. The projection of stars and the extending infinite depth between them on the ceiling is now brutally brilliant and crystalline. His eyes struggle to adjust, squinting and flooding to allow the newly blistering, vivid picture through the burn and into his perception. Each blink calms the sensation until he can stare without strain into the vast artificial universe. His eyes pan from star to star for an amount of time with which he no longer has anything to compare.

Since she came here, he can no longer feign to offer himself even the most inane of calculations to give a definition to this period of non-time. Now things can only happen for as long as they happen. "Now" is all there is, all there may ever be, and eventually, to almost everyone he has ever known, all there ever was. He listens to himself deliberately breathing again, and he closes his eyes.

.   .   .

It is very easy to decide to believe whatever you'd like and to hold fast to that ideology. You can allow your belief to make your decisions for you. But if you can allow for your perspective to change, even in the most hypothetical sense, you'll see a clearer picture of the things you don't or can't understand. While it may cause you incredible internal conflict or force you to make some of the most difficult choices you've ever had to make, the depth of thought you will apply will make everything that much more meaningful. We made IEODs our God, and they are an empty God so now our world is empty. I've lost my faith in that empty God. I hope you will too. I hope you will before you even start. If you do decide to believe in something, decide to believe in something more substantial, something that can evolve with you as you change, even if you have to make it up, hell, especially if you make it up.

I will always wonder if my choice to stay here was the right decision, but so far, each time I step further away from the past, I have only been shown something more beautiful than the clouded memories of time between now and when we all gave ourselves to the ease of familiarity. I will never allow myself to believe that I should be judging Shaffer, the dead girl, or anyone else, but I can tell you, of all the decisions you'll make for yourself, this feels the most right.

•   •   •

8. The Riverside

A cast-iron knocker falls from his hand and bangs against the heavy wooden door one final time as she pulls the door away from him into the house. Her rigid posture guards the darkened entrance.

"Hey, I have a surprise..."

He is interrupted by her taught, tight-lipped face. She looks as though she has been crying. Her eyes avoid his. She pushes her hair behind her ears, sniffles, wipes her reddened nose, and clears her throat.

"...for you."

"Yeah? Um, can you hold on just a minute?" her words scratch through her throat.

She turns and disappears into the house. He is left standing awkwardly near the open door. It is foreign to him to wait here. He can recall pushing his way through this exact door without so much as a momentary hesitation so many times he is unable to count them all. Before it was her house, it was his music library. Before that, it didn't exist, at least not to him, but that seems forever ago.

As she emerges from a far off interior room, he is able to make out the shape of a gun dangling from her fingers. He immediately recalls her skittish exit after taking the pot from his bag. Her change in demeanor after opening his bag seemed like nothing at the time, but now it is mortifyingly obvious. He wonders how he could have been so stupid. A knot grows in his throat as he swells equally with embarrassment and hand-trembling concern.

"Why did you take that? Please, just put it down."

He holds his hand out to her and stumbles backward down the first step off of the porch.

"What the fuck were you doing with this?"

The gun shakes along with her hand as she raises it between them in the doorway.

"You can't take it back, you know? And it won't change a damned thing, but you'll never be the same again. You know that, right?"

Her face accuses him and holds its disdain, continuing to scold him even after her words stop. Her eyes sharpen under her furrowed brow while her upper lip rises, baring her teeth. Darkened strands of red hair stick to trails of tears and scratch down her pale cheeks.

He steps back up onto the porch. A thin smile of calming realization eases his expression of urgent terror. He knows she didn't take it to try to kill herself again, she was trying to protect him from himself. Even though neither of those things were a possibility, the nauseating clench in his gut still grows, but now it is with the certainty that she must be completely aware of the spinning lead following her every motion. Her expression worsens in the light of his obvious relief.

"Oh no! I wasn't going to…"

He stops himself and tries to find words that won't judge her.

"I just found it and I'd never shot one. I mean, I wouldn't. Jesus! I thought that you..."

He hates every word attempting to come out of his mouth as it desperately tries to mask his once more flustered inability to say anything of any use. He is certain his stammering, clumsy attempt to explain is only worsening the situation.

"My God, just stop. I get it."

Her eyes roll, widen, and refocus as she holds the gun out to him.

"Take it, please."

He extends his palm to the gun, and she drops it into his hand. Her arms cross over her chest. Her face is equally embarrassed and irritated as she looks at the ground, just slightly away from him. She turns and begins to walk back into the house. Her abrupt stop to the conversation and the fact that she is no longer holding the gun relieves him slightly, but having the gun in his hands fills him with an entirely new set of sickening anxieties.

"Just let me grab my shoes."

All emotion has escaped her voice as if nothing that just happened was real. Her abrupt change of tone makes him immediately feel as though he has imagined the entire scenario. If not for the weight of the gun in his hand, he would believe that his mind had manufactured every nerve-racking moment of the conversation.

Her nonchalant tone continues as she walks further into the house. He desperately thinks of a way to discard the gun. His composure is held outwardly, but he is frantic in his thoughts, wishing the weapon would magically disappear, wishing that he'd never taken it in the first place. It had never been, and would never be of any use to him in this life.

"Surprise, huh? What's with the U-Haul?" the girl asks.

"Uh, yeah."

Her questions register, tearing him back to why he was there in the first place. He turns to see the truck parked in the street while he tucks the gun into his waistband.

Flashing past him, she skips down the steps off of the porch. He pulls her front door closed and hurries to follow her to the truck. He catches up to her in time to open the truck door for her. She climbs into the passenger side. Like a child excited to go for a ride, she jumps onto the seat. Once again, he closes the door behind her. Leaning through the window and resting her chin on her crossed arms, she smiles at him.

"I'm not helping you move a couch, man."

They ride quietly through the town. The gun grinds into his belly, but there is no chance of him allowing it to be in her line of sight again. He ignores the cold stabbing metal and focuses his attention on her hand as it hangs through the open truck window. Her fingers rise and fall, gliding through the air. He watches her in the reflection of the passenger-side mirror. Her eyes wander through the streets and buildings to the sky and down to the racing asphalt. Tangling orange curls whip around the bullet at her temple and into her eyes. She casually pulls the strands away from her face just to have them flail around her fingers, cling back to her expressionless lips, and weave themselves into her eyelashes. She seems unconcerned with any of it.

.　　.　　.

People will say what they will about "the greater good" and their self-righteous understanding of it, but here, "the greater good" is inconsequential. I know I would forgo any chance of there being any sort of future for all creation just for an opportunity to take the bullet away from her temple. This is only after knowing her for what seems to me like an insignificant period of non-time. The fate of the masses seems useless and unimportant compared to the pain of any one of its individuals. For any single person, compassion, in general, must extend from their care for the very particular people who they have come to know personally. Those particular people whom we have come to know can only be more important to us than faceless, nameless humanity. The tortured lives we find around us, the people who have never had a chance to feel that binding grip of caring or have never understood the responsibility of someone caring for them, those ill-fated souls may never have the capacity in this life to play a role which we would deem satisfactory. They need to be cared for the most. Never expect anything for feelings that are your own. Especially never expect love and compassion to be reciprocal, just learn to appreciate when it is, however it is shown.

.   .   .

"Okay, close your eyes." he says.

She pulls herself off of the window frame to look at him.

"Why?"

"Um, because it's a surprise."

She rolls her eyes, lets out a dramatically annoyed sigh, and places her hands over her eyes.

"Happy?" she asks from behind her hands.

"Ecstatic!"

The U-Haul rounds the corner and stops in the shadow of a marquee awning. Dark neon light tubes backed with red sit atop the awning and read "Riverside Cinema." Clear, round, unlit bulbs outline a white, fluorescent panel which highlights plastic letters that spell, "NOW SHOWING, ANNIe HaLL" perfectly centered below the neon sign.

He runs around the front of the truck and opens the

passenger door. He guides her by her elbow down, off of the passenger's seat, and onto the sidewalk.

"Can I open my eyes now?"

"No, wait. It's better if you wait. Stay right here for a second."

Leaving her next to the truck, he rushes to a generator under the marquee and pulls the starter cable. The engine sputters and rolls into a steady idle. Most of the clear bulbs on the marquee and in the reflective gold ceiling of the awning blink, die, and slowly come back to life with their coiled filaments warming to a soft glow. This is where he would have her open her eyes if it could be dark outside, if the world could match his day forgotten home, but the incessant daylight ruins the lighting spectacle that is the outside of the building. It is still quite beautiful though, he thinks.

"Alright, come with me."

He touches the soft skin behind her elbow, pulling her delicately into the entrance. They move through the doorway, onto the dizzying burgundy paisley carpet, past the small glass-encased candies of the concession stand and the Drymouth popcorn machine, and through the gold stanchions and matching, curving rope lines. He pushes through the button tufted, red leather upholstered door and ushers her past him into the room. He allows her to step beyond his reach. She stops as his hand falls off of her arm and back to his side. Behind them, the door swings back, quietly teetering between the two rooms on its hinges. He steps up to her side and pushes her hands down and away from her closed eyes. She smiles excitedly with her eyes still held closed.

"Go ahead, open them!"

Her eyes burst open.

"It's not exactly what you said, but it is pretty close. I mean, it has the gold trim and the velvet curtains."

He points to the crimson drapes.

"And stale popcorn smell," she adds with her voice quieted with the same awe that leaves her mouth hanging open.

"Yeah, I brought the popcorn machine over here from the Drymouth. I could never get the one here to work, but I cleaned this place up and hooked it up to a generator forever ago, even before I moved into the planetarium. I always loved this place. It was unrecognizable when I first came back," he explains.

He watches her eyes as they gloss over and look to the gold embellished red sea of velvet chairs and perfectly flowing drapes washing over every wall. Golden mirrored metal and milk glass sconces radiate soft white light, washing out the wine-colored curtains. As the blaze dies, it gives way and creates smooth curves

117

of black shadow behind each glowing wave of red fabric. Even further away from the sconce, the contrast softens, blending the black and red stripes between each highlight. It regains its stark, clear definition as it approaches the next light where it is completely flooded with the soft white light again. The aural burn against the wall swings attention down the outside aisles to the stage of the ancient renovated playhouse where a still, pale, stark screen hangs suspiciously out of time, surrounded by antique gold fringe.

He continues, "Everything up in the projection booth works. There is even a perfect copy of Annie Hall in the projector. So you even get a little bit of Coney Island through the eyes of Woody Allen. Probably not exactly what you had in mind, but I figured a twitchy, insecure Coney Island is better than no Coney Island at all, right?"

She grabs her mouth with her hands and her body begins to convulse with a deep heaving cry. Her nose reddens. Tears gray as they pour out of her eyes and wash over her mascara. The darkened saline drops onto her hands where it flows into the lines between her fingers and trickles down the backs of her wrists. Muffled throaty yelps whimper through her grasp. He feels as helpless, hopeless, and confused as he did the moment he met her. His embarrassment in the face of this emotion cements him in panic.

118

She pulls the sleeve of her tee-shirt from her shoulder and wipes her eyes with it. He watches as her face strangles itself back into quiet composure with a sniffle and a forced, pained swallow. A dry-throated, unsteady, creaking laugh sneaks out of her. Shaking, glassy wells of tears collect in her eyes and threaten to spill over, onto her cheeks, but her growing sneer pushes them back into place. She continues to laugh through her words as she sniffs again, wipes her nose, and looks away from him.

"I know what you're thinking. Poor little suicide girl! Maybe if I pretend it's not there she'll feel normal. Right? Well, let me tell you something, you arrogant son of a bitch..."

Her wavering voice corrects itself as she turns to him. Her words are sharp hissing acid.

"...I feel bad for you. That's right! I feel bad for you. You're the sad sack, poor, dumb mother fucker. You think your friend Shaffer's life is pretend? Well, take a look around, asshole..."

The sneering grin falls off of the corners of her lips silencing her sardonic laugh. All that is left are the grinding teeth bared between her tight-lipped anger. He remains struck-still and cannot find a word to pull from his sinking guts. Her hard, thin, accusing finger cuts through the stagnant air as her hand gestures at him, to all directions of the room, and back at him.

"... This, this is not what this town looks like. This town is shit, it's been shit for a long time, and it will always be shit. If you think cleaning up a couple of storefronts and fixing up an old shithole movie theater makes this place as wonderful as your distorted, bullshit, childhood memory of it, then you're dead fucking wrong..."

She accents her points with questioning arm flails. Her eyes narrow as if she's searching his blank face for answers to her shouted rhetorical questions.

"... You pretend to sleep. You pretend that some lights on a ceiling in a dark room can make it night. Your whole fucking miserable existence is pretend. Do you think you're better than your friend, Shaffer, because you stay here? Do you think you're better than me just because you haven't tried to blow your useless fucking brains out? Or do you just think you're above everyone and everything? Why don't you just say it? Say that's what you think. Just fucking say it!"

Her mouth hangs open, ready, begging for some response that it can immediately override with screaming wit. He begs his throat to let out his words.

"I'm sorry."

His mouth cannot form the end of the sentiment before it is interrupted by her angry, irritated scoffing. She turns her side to him and looks to the floor. Her red curls shadow her face while she whispers her words through a desperate laugh.

"Sorry? You're fucking sorry?"

Her head tilts to the ceiling, spilling her hair off of her blushed cheeks. As he stares at her tilted profile, the tears that once clung to her eye now pour out over her temple. She clears her throat with a strained, abrasive cough. Her face slowly returns to parallel her body. Her voice is clear, low, and exact.

"Fuck you!"

She walks away from him without looking for his reaction.

He has lost the cool detachment he felt the last time something like this happened to him. This time he is different. This time the girl is different. This time he cares. He wishes he was able to stop her from leaving, to convince her that he doesn't pity her, to stop her from being angry.

She awkwardly steps, hastily laboring up the incline of the theater aisle in her chrome heels. She stops just short of the door but does not turn back to him.

"You aren't more stable than I am or anyone else is for that matter. You aren't safe from this. It's not depression that made me do this. It was disappointment, the disappointment that hope gave me."

Her voice is soft. She forces her words through a weakened cry. In his own lungs, he can feel her laboring to push the words out of her chest. He can see her back heaving to give her the air needed to speak again.

"All of that bullshit fucking hope."

Her arms swing forward. Her hand accents her last word as it slams through the theater door and blasts it into the lobby. The door swings back and forth, into the theater behind her, out into the lobby, and back, revealing time-lapsed pictures of her further away each time the door opens. He watches the still pictures of her as she pushes through the lobby door and into the street outside. She still does not look back.

The swinging door comes to a rest. Once again, he is alone with his irritated afterthoughts, punishing himself with endless alternate scenarios in which his responses are decent, kind, and not entirely useless. In these scenarios, she does not despise him, and he does not despise himself. If it were possible to truly change the outcome in this reality, he would go back in time as many times as it took, just like Shaffer has, and he would change his reaction until it was perfect.

.   .   .

Mistakes cannot be taken back, that is the danger in actually living, the fear that will handcuff you when you are older, "wiser," and so miserably compassionate that you are too terrified to say something because it might break someone you care about. This is the fear that will make you too uncertain to commit to something that cannot be changed, the fear that will drive you and the rest of the world to give in to the safety of living lives which allow for everything to be malleable and easily changed into something more pleasing.

I mentioned that now when you fuck up, it means more. I feel like it should. It means more now because I chose to make it mean something again. It certainly no longer has to. To fate, we have all been dead for a long time.

Would she go back now if she could? I wonder if you will still want to go back, knowing what you will know after you read this, if you read this. I wonder if this might steal the peaceful ignorant abandon of your youth. I do not wish to stop you from doing and saying things that I would be afraid to, it can be much more regretful to not say or do anything at all. I only want you to understand the hesitation. If you allow for your gut reaction to spill out of your mouth without consideration, it is not bravery. If you take a moment to understand the motives and consequences of your words, know that you can be wrong, and then you still resolve to accept and confront them, that is bravery. I am not brave. I hope you can be.

While I choose to stay here, knowing that my actions here can never be taken back, that is the limit to my resolve. I wish better for you if that is possible. This all could very well be a definite construct that will go forever unchanged by any attempt to derail its concrete and interminably prolonged conclusion. Unfortunately, my inability to accept that it is that way makes it no less a possibility.

Before I could tell her that I did not pity her, I had to consider that maybe I did. I thought I was protecting her from having to relive something that she must be reliving every moment. It was impossible. It was selfish. It was a lie. The truth is I was too uncomfortable to ask her about it because I can't bear to empathize with those emotions any more than I already do. She doesn't need sympathy. She is beyond the scared, feeble, fading optimism I cling to, the optimism with which she must be sickeningly familiar.

She's right, I am the desperate one. I was a little bit right too, I am sorry. You cannot truly care for a person if you are misguided enough to think you are in a position to pity them. No one needs to be pitied, it helps nothing. If you want to help, just care and do the things you know you should do when you care, even if it might break their heart, even if it crushes your own. Do what I now feel incapable of doing and if your intentions are meaningful, just hope that will be enough.

There is sometimes a window in which two people's understanding aligns, and those two people are allowed to see their common thread in this existence. These windows are as rare as they are fleeting. These common understandings, shared points of view, and overlapping standpoints pass as quickly as they arrive, and then they fade even more quickly into obscurity. Those people at those specific times will never leave you if you allow them to stay. They are worth remembering. At the very least, they are worth trying not to forget. I wish she could have known me when I first came back to the theater. Even though no time has passed since then, I was a different person.

•   •   •

9. The Joke

He struggles to pull the wheels of the popcorn machine over the small rise of the door frame threshold. The glass box and wheelbarrow style handles thump and rattle against the door closing on them. His knuckles grind against the brass door handle.

"Son of a fucking bitch!"

His nostrils widen with irritation as he huffs and drops the wooden handles to inspect his hand. He forces a deep breath, grabs back onto the cart, and yanks the machine. The red wagon wheeled base of the machine scratches and gouges into the door. The varnish of the door is scarred with red paint. His body leans as he pulls harder. The machine breaks free of the door. As his grip on the handles slips, his body thumps onto the tile floor.

"Goddamn it."

He grunts as he pushes his body up off of the floor.

The machine indignantly squawks and rumbles as he maneuvers it into the oil-stained corner next to the door. The wheels line up perfectly with the worn marks in the tile. This is where it has been since he can remember and obviously so much longer before then. He plugs it back into the wall, solely for the sake of posterity. The heat lamp at the top of the glass case didn't go out when he unplugged it in the first place. It hasn't as much as blinked since the Pause.

He walks behind the bar, takes a bottle of beer from the cooler, and grabs a random bottle and a small rocks glass from the shelf without looking. He slides onto the stool next to Shaffer's empty seat and places the bottles and glass onto the bar. His hand reaches for Shaffer's abandoned cigarettes and Zippo lighter. He pulls a cigarette from the pack and raises the Zippo to his face. The kitchen door slams against the corner of the bar. His entire body jumps away from the direction of the noise as the Zippo falls to the floor and clinks open. Shaffer stands in the doorway wearing only plaid boxers and a white tee shirt.

"Jesus fucking Christ, Shaffer! You scared the shit out of me."

"Who the hell are you?" Shaffer feigns the shock and concern of an elderly woman happening upon an intruder, wearing only her unmentionables.

The smaller man shakes his head in disapproval as he stares at Shaffer.

"Boy, Shaf, that joke just never really gets old, does it?"

Shaffer tries to hold back a laugh, but it turns into a nasal gag of air as it works its way out through the teeth of his infectious grin. His voice cracks to an unnaturally high pitch as he speaks.

"Ah, man!"

Shaffer wipes his eye as if it's watering due to the overwhelming hilarity of his joke.

"No, it never really does." Shaffer responds with his voice cracking again.

Amused relief takes over the look of startled terror on the smaller man's face. He shakes his head and bends down to pick up the lighter.

"Shaf, why are you not wearing pants?"

He lights his cigarette and prepares for what he knows will be, at its very least, an interesting response.

"I'm not wearing pants because, fuck you! Why the fuck not? The question is why are you wearing pants? I mean, look the fuck around, my friend."

Shaffer's arms raise and spread to their full, epic wingspan.

His body twists to the left, to the right, and back to the center as if he is accepting applause from a crowd of millions of clamoring imaginary fans all standing and applauding the sight of his hairy legs. He puts his massive hands to his mouth to project his already blasting voice.

"NOBODY, FUCKING NOBODY!"

He lets his arms flop back to his sides.

"See, I doubt it will offend anyone. By the way, if you were thinking about making a Manhattan, you're missing almost all the ingredients."

"What?" the smaller man is confused by the question.

"You're like the worst drinker ever. Were you planning on having sweet vermouth, straight? What the fuck is wrong with you?" He turns to look to where Shaffer is pointing.

"Damn! I wasn't paying attention. I just grabbed the closest thing."

"You must be out of it. You also only grabbed one glass. I have fucking feelings, you know?"

Shaffer's bare feet slap against the tile as he makes his way around the bar. He slides open the under-bar cooler door and inspects the contents.

"Well, there are no bitters, but let's be honest, you don't

really need any more bitter. Let's make them the only way I like them."

He pulls out a gallon container of Maraschino Cherries.

"Sweet, very sweet and very red."

He drops the plastic jug of red syrup and fruit on the bar top next to the sweet vermouth.

"For this, we'll need the cheap bourbon."

He shuffles through the stainless steel well hanging from the ice bins and sinks. The bottles clink together as he lifts them, one by one, eyeing each label and allowing them to crash back into the well before he picks up the next. He pulls a bottle to eye level and inspects it in the light.

"Ah, yes! This is the one. The cheaper, the sweeter."

Shaffer flips the lid of the ice maker open and fills two rocks glasses with ice chunks. He pours sweet vermouth, bourbon, and a splash of cherry juice into each glass. The ice chunks fall, splashing and spilling the cocktails as he dumps them into a steel tumbler and back into the glasses. He drops three cherries and two tiny black straws into each glass.

The smaller man quietly looks on through the curling sidestream cigarette smoke rising from the ashtray. The cherries slowly tumble through the ice chunks to the bottom of the drinks on the bar. He looks up to see Shaffer's meaty hand dwarfing the rocks glass as he pushes it through the cigarette smoke to him. He picks up the dark red concoction and taps it against Shaffer's.

"To the impossibility of hangovers."

"Whatever you say, Shaf. You do know I can see your nipples through that shirt, right?"

He sips the drink and feels himself relax into the sweet whiskey burn rolling down through his chest. An uncontrollable gag reflex chokes him. He coughs to clear his throat of the warming sugary coating. He sets the nearly full glass back on the bar while Shaffer keeps his own drink to his lips. The black straws in Shaffer's glass are held, bent over the side of the glass, and wedged between his index and middle finger. His hand is too large to allow his pinky finger to rest on the glass. The shortest and most adorably proper of his thick fingers slightly rises from the rest of his hand as he continues to tip the cocktail. The ice chunks fall against his teeth and the last of the red liquid disappears. He shakes the glass against his open mouth allowing in some ice and two of the cherries. The ice crunches between his molars. His glass knocks onto the bar while he questions the smaller man.

"What, you don't like it?" Shaffer asks defensively.

"The drink, or being able to see your nipples?"

"The drink. My nipples are majestic, everyone knows that."

132

"It's fine, I don't hate it at all."

"IT'S FINE?"

Shaffer grabs the drink away and scowls at the smaller man.

"It's fine… You ungrateful son of a…" he mumbles, raising the glass to his face.

The drink vanishes as quickly as the first. Shaffer forces a preposterously satisfied noise from the back of his throat and grins staring at the empty glass.

"Hey, I was going to drink that!"

"Yeah, but you wouldn't have enjoyed it the way I do. You know, the right way."

Shaffer grabs a beer from the cooler and the beer from in front of his friend. He removes both caps at the same time with the edge of the bar and a smack of his thick hand. He slides one of the beers across the bar.

"You're right. I don't think anyone has ever enjoyed anything as much as you enjoyed those two drinks. How long were you back there this time? I didn't think I'd be seeing you so soon here."

"Dude, I've been back here several times since the last time I saw you. Christ, one of the trips, I was back there for like eight years!"

Shaffer pulls two more beers out of the cooler and walks around the bar.

"Jesus, I had no idea. Seems like I saw you a couple of days ago. Eight years though, wow man! You were with her for eight years without being an asshole once?"

"Well thank you so much for being so fucking surprised that it's not impossible for me to not be an asshole."

Shaffer's eyes widen as he speaks. His voice raises and his head wobbles, pretending that his feelings have been compromised. His overly animated nature doesn't allow for him to be taken seriously, sometimes even if he is being serious. The smaller man senses that Shaffer is joking, as usual, and he begins to laugh.

"Sorry man. So, eight years with her! Great job, bud."

"Nah, I was only actually with her for a couple of hours. I decided to tell her exactly what was actually going on. Like, I traveled back in time, I know everything about you, I've been doing this for a very long time, your favorite color is yellow, yadda, yadda, yadda. Needless to say, it didn't go as I planned it."

"So you diner scene'd her? You Bill-fucking-Murray-diner-scene'd her and it didn't work? Fucking excellent! Now I don't even know what is right or wrong anymore."

They both laugh.

"So, what did you do with the other seven years, three hundred and sixty-four days, and twenty-two hours?"

"I roadied for Bruce Springsteen."

"Get the fuck out of here! The fucking Boss? Damn it, that's awesome!"

Shaffer leans back in his seat and crosses his arms smugly.

"Yep, it is awesome. That's exactly what it is."

"So, did you ever make it past Katie's sister's wedding reception?"

"Kind of, it took a couple more trips. Man, that guy just doesn't get Pearl Jam! It felt so good punching him in his ignorant face."

Shaffer looks up to the ceiling while sipping his beer and obviously reveling in the satisfying memory.

"Jesus, Shaf, you punched the guy in his face at his own wedding reception?"

"Hell yeah! I went to jail that time. The next time I went back, I just faked having the flu, so I didn't have to go to the wedding."

"Solid move, but you're obviously here again so, what happened that time?"

"I couldn't just let it go. I knew he would have said it if I had been there. Just knowing that he thought it was too much for me to ignore. I punched him as soon as they got back from their honeymoon."

"Well, if nothing else, you should be commended for your restraint. That must have been really difficult for you."

"Yeah, right? I mean, the guy really is an ass."

They toast their bottles once more. The glass clinks with the tone of approval. They both sip through sarcastic smirks.

"You know, Shaf, to this day, you are still the only person I've ever really punched in the face."

"Really? I don't recall you ever hitting me. No worries though, I was probably blackout drunk and most likely deserved it."

"Shaffer, you were sitting right over there. You were definitely wasted, but I know you remember. I didn't hit you out of anger, you actually begged me to hit you as hard as I could in your face. I remember it like it was yesterday, it was the night before Thanksgiving so the bar was packed. "Rearview Mirror" was playing on the jukebox, and we were drinking dollar domestics. I have no idea why you wanted me to hit you, but you wouldn't let it drop so finally I hit you. You don't remember?"

Shaffer grimaces apologetically, shrugs his shoulders, and shakes his head.

"Sorry man, I got nothing."

Shaffer being blacked out would be a perfectly logical excuse except that they had rehashed this story more times than the smaller man can remember. This was their mutually favorite reminiscing story. The smaller man feels gutted. This time it is not a classic Shaffer, time travel-induced, memory loss joke. Shaffer had made this joke several times, but never with such a straight face. A part of their relationship and common understanding has been erased. The smaller man feels the sweet warm bourbon in his belly climbing back up into his throat as his stomach turns. He used to hate it when Shaffer faked this scenario. Now, he would do just about anything to be able to pretend to himself that Shaffer was kidding, prodding at the irrational fear of losing their past. The smaller man and his nauseated stomach know that his wishes are as worthless as it would be to try to jog Shaffer's memory. The garbage man is now the lone keeper of this discarded garbage memory.

"So where's PEEW!"

Shaffer mimics shooting himself in the temple with his

137

finger. The smaller man breaks from his daze to find Shaffer obviously, nervously trying to change the subject. He looks at Shaffer's face and it is clear that Shaffer knows just as well as he does that the memory is gone.

"Ah, yeah, um, I don't think she's doing too well."

"Well, I'd say! She fucking shot herself in the head for Christ's sake!"

Shaffer jumps back into dark, nervous humor. The smaller man is gracious for the distraction and hopes they can find a place in the conversation to forget the awkward unspoken understanding that, at the very least, a small piece of their history has been replaced in Shaffer's mind. He nods at Shaffer, tries to force a smile, and waits for the lump in his tight throat to subside.

"So, what were you doing skulking around in the kitchen with no pants?" the smaller man asks.

"I was looking for something salty to have with my beer because someone stole the GODDAMNED POPCORN MACHINE!"

"Oh, yeah, I borrowed it for a little while."

"I know. I watched you struggling to get it back through the door."

"What? That was a total pain in the ass. I bashed my hand.

Why didn't you come and help?"

"Well fuck, I think you answered your own question. That didn't look like any fun at all."

Shaffer's words are broken by a half-evil thundering belly laugh and half-smoker's cough. His eyes actually water this time as he coos between chuckles and wipes away the tears.

"Fucking hilarious, Shaf! You're a real friend."

"Well, I guess that will learn ya from stealing shit."

"I took it over to the theater."

"Why?" Shaffer asks.

"Because I wanted to surprise the girl. She mentioned she likes theaters."

Shaffer's face bends out of shape with confusion.

"WHY?" he asks again.

"Because, fucking popcorn goes with going to the movies!"

"No, I mean why are you here, trying to impress this girl? It's not like you're going to fuck her, not here. I mean, it's impossible to even want to. Hell, even if it were possible, I imagine it would be pretty fucking difficult with that bullet spinning right next to her. That shit is distracting, I could hardly look away."

The smaller man sighs and grins at Shaffer's ability to completely forgo any modicum of his emotional maturity for the sake of amusement, especially if it is only to amuse himself. Still, the smaller man cannot help but laugh and shake his head. He knows Shaffer means nothing by it.

"You're such an asshole."

Shaffer shrugs his shoulders as he spins away from the bar on his stool. He responds while he walks to the popcorn machine.

"Well, YEAH! But seriously though, I get your reasoning for staying here, even if it is nuttier than squirrel shit, and I get trying to find some company, but why would you drag a popcorn machine all the way across town to impress someone when there is absolutely no need to?"

He sets two full bowls of popcorn on the bar in front of them.

"Honestly?" the smaller man asks.

"Sure, not that I could give a shit, but for the sake of conversation, yeah, honestly?"

"I'm pretty sure she's stuck here, and she's probably not ecstatic about that, as you so eloquently put, 'she fucking shot herself in the head for Christ's sake.' I just wanted her to feel like she belongs somewhere. I thought that if she felt satisfied with the way it can be here she might not have to think about why she did what she did, or why she wanted to do what she did. Maybe she could forget for a little while."

"I don't know, man," Shaffer responds, "I don't think anybody belongs here. I only kept going back because, what the fuck, man, what else was I going to fucking do? Now, I actually like it. Back then, that's where I belong. I could be wrong, man, maybe you do belong here. Fuck, on the increasingly rare occasion that you are here, I like seeing you in between my trips, so I am totally cool with you being here. As a matter of fact, I'm fucking tickled when I do get to see you. But the choice to go back or stay here is definitely a one or the other thing. There is no third option. You can't just refuse to participate. Honestly though, you do have to at least consider that maybe she does think she has it figured out for her, maybe she doesn't want to belong back then or now. She decided she belongs dead. Maybe she thinks that actually is what's best for her. Regardless, there's not a damned thing anyone can do to change it now. Unfortunately, for her, being dead is still not an option."

"Well, it didn't work at all. I don't even know if she will ever want to see me again."

Shaffer grins and smacks the smaller man's back.

"That's too bad. She was excellent at picking music on the jukebox. If it's any consolation to you, I do feel way better now

141

that the popcorn machine is back where it belongs."

.   .   .

Just before time travel afforded us the possibility of escape, people were as divided as we had ever been. There were those who believed anyone not distinctly and exactly like them were evil, and there were those who believed that nothing about any of us was evil, that evil didn't actually exist. That singular separation created innumerous lines of division that went well beyond that initial disagreement. Varying degrees of each line of logic on either side shattered the common bonds of our existence like a wrecking ball through tempered glass. When we were growing up we figured not giving up on ourselves was the last hold we had to hope, it turns out that what was actually keeping all of this together was not giving up on other people. Hell, I guess we were all a little bit right.

What was more damning was that we collectively refused to believe or accept our true commonalities, that we were all at least a little bit evil and, more importantly, we were all almost completely wrong. If you can't accept that there's evil in the world, it will destroy you. You will suffer the same fate if all you see is evil.

Wanting to be away from the present is the great equalizer. Differences are nearly extinct. The things that we were, the people we thought we were, the opinions we believed to be paramount, sex, race, politics, none of it matters, it never really did. Now, the only real defining line of division is that you are here in the Pause or you are somewhere in the past. It doesn't matter what you want or think or disagree with or hate or love. You are here or you are not.

.　　　.　　　.

He cringes, shields his eyes, and stumbles onto the sidewalk. The glass of the Drymouth Tavern door flashes with the reflection of the sun as the door closes behind him. Blinding light surrounds him. The entire street is whitewashed from his view. He lights a cigarette as the town comes back into focus. He trips into the street past the U-Haul and turns to walk along the double yellow lines. He stops as he comes to the intersection.

In his head, a harmonica cries out sad chilling notes of sentimental dusty Midwest Americana by way of New Jersey and Shaffer's bold tone takes the lead with Bruce Springsteen singing backup vocals to "Thunder Road." He looks to the right, down the street that leads to the planetarium, the streets he walked to the

Drymouth with the dead girl. In his mind he pictures Shaffer belting out the lyrics, he smiles and looks down at his feet. Something about combining booze and Springsteen always felt like raw honesty, it always made him feel as though whatever moment he was in was something epic and defining. It always made him feel young. The feeling quickly fades into self-deprecating embarrassment as it always has, as defeating maturity has forced it to.

He looks back up, to the left, in the direction of the dead girl's house. He turns right and walks toward home with Shaffer still shouting the Springsteen song in his mind.

.   .   .

You can get so used to fighting for everything that it becomes your definition of life. That is part of the empty feeling now. How can you bring yourself to accept that you don't need to fight anymore? You'll ask yourself countless times if this is your own psychosis. What if the true reason you can no longer go back is that you are holding onto a time when you needed to fight because it was your reality for so long that now nothing seems real unless you are struggling? What if you really are the one living in the past? What if everything you do is all bullshit and time travel is

144

actually fucking heaven, but you just can't bring your fucking self to accept it so you are damned to be miserable for fucking ever? There aren't any answers. I'd like to tell you that, eventually, you'll stop asking yourself, but this will become your new fight, your new infinite and imperative struggle. It either satisfies your need for an antagonist or allows you to continually convince yourself that your reality is reality, either way, you will come to understand faith.

Regardless of the terms or what might define that faith, it is a blind belief that how you feel is real and it is important. If nothing else, that understanding allows you to understand how essential everyone else's emotions are, how significant their beliefs are, however unlike yours that they may be. Unfortunately, as you can clearly see by what I have shared with you, as much as you will ever understand any of this, you will never truly know what it is to be someone else. I'm not sure how anyone could begin to think that they do understand someone else. For most, if not all, of our lives it's impossible to even understand ourselves. After having lived through more non-time than you can possibly imagine, more existence than I can still comprehend, I feel no further along in this pursuit than I ever have. Each thing that I have learned has only shown me a million more things that I may never understand.

.   .   .

He is still, sitting at the desk. His hands hover over the keyboard painting bold, black shadows onto the typewriter. Half-rolled into the typewriter on the desk, a glowing white page reflects the light from the lamp above him onto his face. A thin, perfect string of smoke rises straight up, completely undisturbed, from an ashtray on the desk. His eyes lose focus between his fingers, and his vision drifts into the gaps between the keys. The keys fall beneath his fingers. The steel bars smack against the page as it turbulently jerks to the left between the punctuation of each snapping letter. His hands pull away from the keys. He reaches for the cigarette and leans back against the desk chair. The thin string of smoke swings back to his face with his hand, and he takes a drag. His eyes focus up into the dark room on the line of light outlining the side door. He glances around to the almost entirely shadowed bookshelf, record player, and couch.

.   .   .

You aren't really going back. If from the moment you get there you are creating a new reality, how can that new reality be yours? It belongs to the people that remain there once you are gone. This probably applies to anyone's reality.

146

This is all beginning to feel like a game to me, and we have figured out a way to cheat it so that we have a countless number of these meaningless lives. How can we really care about any of them or anyone in them when we know we can simply start again whenever we want to? All of those fucking people, how can they just be throwaways? We are so detestably cavalier with their existence that even time has abandoned us. IEODs may have been our empty God, but we became something worse, something detached, we are the careless, terrible Gods to the past. We care so little for them that we have no concern about the fact that they may actually have to go on in the fractured realities we have created for them, simply so that we can be distracted, just so that we can be amused.

You can't go back to your life, it's not yours anymore. If you want to do something or change something you can really only do it now. Allow the past to change you, allow it to influence you to do what you think is right, right now. Don't only ask, "What have we done?" there are better questions.

.   .   .

He leans back over the typewriter. A cigarette hangs from his lip. His fingers hesitate at the keys as he looks down to find the words. He types a few more sentences and rests his index finger on the period key. Bits of ash fall slowly down through the gaps between the keys. His eyes move to the page as he continues to try to find the words he has yet to write. His index finger remains on the period key while his other hand takes the cigarette from his mouth and stubs it out in the ashtray. He looks back down to his finger and traces the heart-shaped outline of the key. The weight of his hand relaxes. His finger delicately pushes the key into the machine. The keybar cracks against the paper and falls back into place leaving an ink stain dot to the right of the last word he typed. He pulls the sheet from the top of the machine and leans back into the desk chair once more. He looks over the fresh type and places it face-down onto the stack of pages in the letter tray on the floor.

He slides out of the desk chair. As he walks toward the couch, his hand reaches back to twist the switch on the top of the lamp. The switch clicks and the desk and typewriter are gone into the darkness. He eases his body onto the couch and curls onto his side. Stars hang ignored in his periphery. He looks into the blank blackness and closes his eyes.

•   •   •

10. The Roller Coasters, The Beach, and The Cotton Candy

"Don't you know that when a girl storms off you're supposed to follow her and grovel until she finds something that you say accidentally amusing? Then she laughs at you, you get embarrassed, and everything is better?"

His eyes pop open with her first word. His body jerks into a startled stiff sit-up with his hands grasping to the couch cushion and backrest as his foot kicks the floor. The quick scare vanishes in the same manner with which it came.

"Jesus Christ!"

His hands loosen their grip as his leg slides off of the couch, and he pushes his body to sit upright. Her silhouette leans with its hip against the frame and its arms crossed in the bright doorway.

"Would it have made any difference?" he asks.

"Well, no!" she scoffs.

They push their voices to resonate through the distance between them. He stands and walks to the lighting console. A dim band of light just slightly brightens the room as it rises onto the dome ceiling. The room warms to the last minute of what the end of a sunset used to be, just enough for him to make out her facial features. His hand pulls away from the controls.

"Do you ever enter a room with someone in it and not scare the shit out of them? I don't get a lot of visitors now, but I seem to remember something about people knocking on doors a long time ago."

He smiles widely to make sure that she knows he isn't being serious.

"Oh! Sorry, mister sensitive! Would you have been any less startled if I had pounded on the door?"

He flops back onto the couch. The tattered leather puffs around him. He speaks with feigned childish obstinance while the cushions exhale back to their normal state.

"Probably not."

She steps onto the ramp landing and allows the door to gently close behind her. She leans her back against the inside of the door. Her head tilts upward to the ceiling and the stars now faded in the low light. He can feel the awkwardness of her purposefully diverted attention. He follows suit, looking up at the dome as to not pressure her to meet his eyes.

"Um, yeah, so I just wanted to come and say goodbye."

"You're leaving?"

His voice jumps embarrassingly.

She puts her fist to her mouth and clears her throat.

"Ahem, um yeah, but I kind of really felt like shit for being such a bitch to you and I didn't want what I said to be the last thing I said to you. I wanted to say I'm sorry. I know you were just doing something nice."

Her face sheepishly points down as she speaks. The heel of her right silver pump fidgets with the shiny, sharp-pointed toe of the left.

"Do you want a drink?"

He stands and gestures to the bookshelf next to him where a bottle of bourbon sits next to two empty glasses in front of the books.

"Sure."

She pushes herself off the door and walks down the ramp.

The glasses clink together as he picks them up off of the shelf.

"Where will you go?" he asks.

His tone is purposefully even and quieted as she comes nearer. He pours the bourbon into the two short rocks glasses wedged between his fingers. He holds them out to her.

"What?"

She takes one of the glasses from his hand.

"You just said you're leaving. Where are you going?"

"Oh yeah, I guess I don't really know, just not here."

Her face hangs down toward her drink. She rolls the brown liquor around the thick bottom of the glass. The glass rises to her bottom lip. She tips her head back. The bourbon slides quickly away from the bottom of the glass and every drop disappears into her mouth. She grazes her grimacing bottom lip with her knuckle, wiping away the cool evaporating alcohol. Her eyes close while she obviously forces herself to push the burning mouthful of booze down her throat. As her eyes open, they flood. Pleasantly noxious alcohol-laced breath eases out of her mouth with a whimper. Immediately, she pushes the glass back to him, and he pours two more fingers of bourbon into it.

"Roller coasters, cotton candy, and the beach?" he questions her with his grin and sips his drink.

She steps around him to the couch.

"Yeah, maybe."

She hunches down, takes off her heels, and sits on the floor with her back against the couch. Her white feet press against the floor in front of her tightly folded legs. Behind her knees, on her lap, she fidgets with her glass. He moves to the other end of the couch, squats down, and labors to get his body seated. His crossed feet slip from under him dropping him the last inches to the floor. His drink spills over the glass and onto his hand. The bourbon audibly sloshes around inside the bottle as he thumps against the floor and the couch. He checks to see if she is watching the awkward mess, but she has not looked up from her lap. He settles himself and sips his drink again.

"Sit much?" she casually asks without as much as a glance in his direction.

A laugh bursts through his lips leaving him choking on the small sip of bourbon that has yet to make it all the way down his throat. He turns to see the corners of her lips fighting off a smile. She continues to look away maintaining her composure, but he can see her nostrils flaring to hold back the laughter. An impish pride glows on her face.

"You know, I know there isn't much of a difference, right? I get that everything that I've done here only shows that I am just as obsessed with the past as anyone else is. It is just as difficult for me as I imagine it is for anyone else to accept this as life. I know why they go back and I completely understand not wanting to be here at all. Everything you said was right. You didn't need to apologize."

"How long ya been working on that?" she asks.

Her question flushes him with embarrassment. She smiles an apology for making fun of him.

She turns her head and rests her chin on her shoulder. Her face is straight. He can see her eyes searching the floor between them for the right words as she speaks.

"Life doesn't need for us to accept it, it goes on even without time, and we can't choose to be a part of it or apart from it any more than we were ever able to, but time, time needs us. I know what you are saying, and I appreciate it."

She pulls her chin up off of her shoulder and continues, "Can we be done with the apologies and acceptance speeches?"

Her face begs him for something more casual, something more like the way they were able to speak before the theater, before he realized she took the gun, before he was forced to acknowledge that they both knew there was a bullet spinning next to her, just waiting for time to need her again. He sips his drink and wonders how two such accomplished pretenders could possibly struggle this much to act the way they did before any of this. Knowing that they can never be those people again empties him in the same way as Shaffer losing their shared memory did. She extends her glass to him. He reaches the bottle out to her and pours it backhanded into her glass.

"Sure thing."

He forces his face into an easy smile. They sit silently. He knows there isn't anything more to say, at least not that she would want to hear or talk about. His gaze parallels hers, off into the dim warm glow of the beginning of the domed ceiling, just above the shining outline of the emergency exit standing over the room. He lights his last two cigarettes to busy his hands. He holds one of the cigarettes out to her, and she accepts it. They both look back to the farthest point in the ceiling. While they smoke and sip their bourbon in silence, the thick hum of the room returns to his perception. He is more aware of the crushing tonal pressure than he has ever been. He can only focus on the weight he feels compressing his chest. As the crescendoing orchestral noise in his head grows, it surrounds him. He feels himself shrinking into the commanding reverberation.

The clack of her empty glass against the wooden bookshelf shakes him from the inexorable hold of his delusion. Lucid clarity interrupts the sound, the pressure, and his panic. She stubs her finished cigarette out in an ashtray on the lighting console.

"Thank you, for umm, everything."

She blows out her last lungful of smoke between her nervous words.

"I'm going to go now."

"Will I see you again before you leave?" he asks.

He waits with his full attention on her and what she will say in response. The clean, clear direction of thought causes him more dread than the deafening, constrictive torture that came before it.

"Yeah, I mean, maybe. I don't really know."

She crosses her arms over her stomach and stares at the floor just in front of his feet. As he pushes himself up off of the floor, she quickly turns away.

"So, yeah, okay. Umm, maybe I'll see you some other time."

Her postured voice falters as she walks away glancing over her shoulder. She flashes him a giant trembling smile as she grabs the railing and turns up the ramp. He can see the sad desperation in her tearing eye and blushed nose and cheeks. She winks and half-waves without slowing her gait. His hand rises to wave back, but her head is turned away, and she is to the door before he can respond. The silhouette of her body almost disappears into the burn of the sunlight before the door closes behind her.

He considers running to catch her, but he immediately feels selfish for even thinking of trying to get her to stay. His body mindlessly drifts in front of the desk and falls into the chair. He stretches to reach the lighting controls. The room goes black again under the convincing night sky. He pours the last of the bourbon into his glass and lets the bottle slip from his hand onto the floor.

Reflections of light from the gap around the door and the night sky dance in his glass with the whiskey. He sips the drink and watches the lights float in the liquor. He thinks of nothing for as long as his mind allows it. The last sip of bourbon and the glowing reflections empty into his mouth. He reaches for the bottle on the floor. Stars shine through the empty whiskey fifth as he holds it up to the ceiling. He stands and tosses the bottle into the shadows. Feeling his way through the dark rows of seats, he makes his way to the bright outline of the door. The stars fade. Light rolls over him as he pushes through the door and drops the unplugged extension cord onto the cement.

He kills the generator on his way to the replica motorcycle. His leg swings over the seat, and he pulls the bike off its stand. He drops onto the machine, pushing through the kickstart. The bike turns over and quickly dies. He repositions himself and tries again. With the full weight of his body, his foot pushes through the kickstart twice more with no response from the engine. He pulls his leg back over the bike and pushes it back up onto its stand. His hand checks his jacket pocket for a cigarette and finds the flat empty pack he left there.

"Mother fuck!"

The empty pack balls up in his fist, and he throws it at the bike. His hands smack against the seat and gas tank. He grunts as his body strains to slowly tip the motorcycle. His weight nearly follows the bike to the ground forcing him to stumble and jump over the bike to keep his balance. He catches his footing and looks back at the bike to see the white rabbit's foot swinging from the ignition. In front of the rabbit's foot, on the ground lies the crumpled cigarette pack. He looks at the small piece of trash, grits his teeth, and turns to walk toward the Drymouth. He takes a few steps and guilt pulls him to a stop. Warm sick nausea turns his stomach and his body back to the motorcycle. He kneels down to the cigarette pack, picks it up, flattens it out, and pushes it back into his jacket pocket.

• • •

11. The Ghosts and Their Satanic Majesty

The Drymouth feels more abandoned than it ever has. He steps on the shadowed letters, through the light. After the door closes behind him, his footsteps are the only sound in the bar. There have been many times since the Pause that he has visited this place and Shaffer did not appear, but he has never had the feeling that it wouldn't happen. Somehow, this time he knows he will not see him. The normal anxious excitement that he feels sitting at this bar alone, waiting for his friend, is as absent as Shaffer himself.

He pours the cheap bourbon into the glass, both left on the bar from his last visit, and takes his seat at the bar. He reaches down the bar, in front of Shaffer's empty stool, and slides the half-full pack of cigarettes, Zippo, and ashtray to himself. Smoke plumes into the air as he lights a cigarette and laughs to himself at the thought of two Shaffers hanging out together. He reaches his glass out and toasts to Shaffer's empty seat.

"Not even here and still fucking funny!"

The glass empties into his mouth. Standing on the bottom rung of his stool, he reaches over the bar and pulls a bottle back to himself. With his cigarette hanging from his lips, he tucks the new bottle and the cheap bourbon under his arm, pours a few of the cigarettes out of the pack onto the bar next to Shaffer's seat, and shoves the rest of the cigarettes into his jacket pocket.

The Drymouth letters and light from the window bend around his feet and slide up to his chest as he walks to the door.

"Later, Shaf."

The door opens into the street where the U-Haul is just as he left it. He drops the bottles through the cab's open window onto the front passenger's seat next to his backpack. As he walks around the back of the truck, he pushes the ramp back in and pulls the door closed. The clanking metal of the ramp and door latch echo through the barren shop-lined street.

He climbs into the cab and imagines her sitting next to him with her hair wrapping around her face and her hand gliding through the air out of the open window. The engine turns over. His hand spins the wheel as far as it will go and the engine revs out of key with the whining of the power steering. The front passenger's side wheel jumps over the curb on the other side of the street. He stiffens his grip on the steering wheel to keep himself from being jostled around the cabin. The gun slides from under his bag and rests against his leg. The truck pulls to the intersection, and he slams the gearshift into park.

His hand grasps the gun while he throws the door open with his elbow. He walks in front of the running truck to the garbage can at the corner of the sidewalk. The appeal of it is still not entirely lost on him as he holds the gun out in his palm over the trash. He feels the satisfying weight of the weapon, the delicate curve of its grip settling perfectly into the contours of his hand. His fingers open and bend away from him toward the ground allowing the weight of the gun to roll itself off of them and into the garbage. He gets back into the truck and pulls through the intersection turning, this time, toward her house.

.   .   .

The engine dies. He pulls the key from the ignition and leans back into the seat. He grabs a pack of Drymouth matches from the cup holder, lights a cigarette, and looks to her house through the smoke floating out of the open window of the truck cab. From what he can see, aside from the vast library of albums and pictures, the room is vacant. The hash marked sunlight leans against the wall of records, but nothing moves inside of the house. He did not expect her to be there. He has been fighting the hope of seeing her again since she left him alone in the planetarium, yet his eyes continue to strain and focus from the side of the street into the house through the window.

He hates his desperation and the torment of his impossible wish that he had done something or at least tried to do something to make her stay. These thoughts scold him again, and he knows he has not learned from his regret and self-destructive hesitations. His mind wrestles itself. These things didn't even happen in the past, they all happened right now, right here in the Pause, how could he be regretful for something he did or did not do when it is impossible for those things to even be in the past? The pit of useless spiraling reason and logic he has managed to somehow keep his mind from disappearing into now demands him to make sense of what this is, to decide how his thoughts or any of this could matter at all to anyone or anything. He knows there is no satisfying these tortures, no relief from any of it, no hope after allowing himself to believe that this inability to comprehend even his own rationalizations is all there is and all there will ever be.

Mindlessly, his body lets itself out of the truck and carries him to the dark wooden door of her house. The iron of the door knocker clanks three times under the weight of his hand, and he waits for what he is sure will be no response. His knuckles wrap against the door twice more as he presses the latch on the handle and lets himself into the house.

His mind imprints her against the backdrop of the shelves of records, where he saw her for the first time. She is dazed and silent in his memory. Her eye is clouded with smoke. The bullet spins by her temple and follows her as she stands and walks across the room. His feet retrace her steps to the record shelves where the picture that she turned over still lies on its face. He pulls the picture off of the shelf and turns it over in his hand. In the picture, she looks less like herself than he remembers. His reflection in the glass of the picture frame stares back at him. Both he and the reflection are expressionless and dim, darkened by their own shadows. Carefully, he places it back where it originally stood, leaning it on its stand next to the records. The glare from the window reflecting on the glass whites her out of existence in the photograph.

His fingers trace over the spines of the record sleeves. He follows along the shelves through the room passing by her ghost. A few albums fall to their sides, away from his hand. The records slap down onto the shelf. Something that had been wedged between them flashes, flipping through the light coming from the window. It lands on the carpet in front of him. Kneeling down he sees two paper clips fastened together on the floor. He slides them into the breast pocket of his jacket and looks to the fallen records. The last album standing in the row is Their Satanic Majesty's Request, and the back cover of the album lying face down next to it is Sticky Fingers. The paper clips were holding the space of the Rolling Stones record he had borrowed well before he met her. He cannot recall if placing the paper clips between the records was something that he had done. He wonders if she did it.

He pulls the paper clips back out of his pocket, separates them, and places one back onto Their Satanic Majesty's Request. The record sleeves slide along the shelf with the push of his hand. The albums cling back together as he stands them on end and leans them back up against the rest of the row.

She passes by him. He intersects her path just a step behind her as he walks to the door. A memory of his nervous self fumbles over its words, talking to her from the doorway. The memory is gone as he reaches through it to open the door. He turns to see her. As she walks, light from the last window pane falls off of her body and settles, undisturbed against the shelves behind her. Once more, she is gone.

•   •   •

12. The Diminishing Return

He flips the toggle switch on the generator, rests his foot on the machine, and yanks the handle of the pull start. The generator chugs and releases a few puffs of black smoke. He pulls again. The engine quickly races and settles into an even idle. His steps run parallel to the extension cord, following it to the door. He picks up the disconnected end of the cord and pulls the door open. The door opens a few inches and comes to a quick stop with a few clinks of an extended chain attached from the inside. His face is distorted with complete confusion as he stares down at the chain and pulls harder with the same result.

He wedges his face into the opening. A lantern moves toward the door. The dead girl's figure is highlighted behind the glass-covered flame, and she is glowing just enough for him to see that it is her. She disappears from his view through the door. As he continues to stare into the room he can hear her faint sobbing getting louder. She flashes in the stream of light inches away from his face. The flash of her body in the light startles him. As his body recoils away from the door, he can only muster enough presence of mind to shout one word.

"HEY!"

His head swings down in disappointment at his pathetic inability to say anything useful, once again.

"Hey? Come on, man! What the fuck?" he curses himself, whispering into his chest.

His head pushes up and back into the door. He can hear her sniffling and pattern-less sobs fading as she walks farther down the catwalk, around the room, and toward the front doors.

Her distant voice shakes through whimpers and the darkness. The words she speaks are just loud enough for him to hear them over the generator's engine.

"I'm sorry!"

"Wait! What? What are you sorry for?" he shouts through the gap into the black of the planetarium.

He waits for an answer, but he hears nothing except the engine moan and the faint sound of a closing door. He lets the chained door close, and he sprints through the grass around the building. As he rounds the front of the building, he can see her through the glass-paned double doors. She twists the aluminum knob on the interior of the door before he can get to them. His fingers touch the door handle as he hears the distinct metallic clack of the locks bolting into place. He grasps the silver handles and pulls, but the doors just rattle and hold closed. She stares down at the lock while he raps on the glass and yells.

"WHAT ARE YOU DOING? LET ME IN!"

He's not angry, he shouts out of pure confusion. He cannot place any meaning to her actions. She appears pained and tortured. It's as if her entire body is hanging from strings, and she is controlled by something outside of her will. The lantern swings at her knee, her hand labors and shifts to keep a grasp on its handle. Her arm lifts her hand hanging from her limp wrist. She presses her palm against the inside of the glass. She stares at her hand while it creaks down the pane until it is directly opposite his pounding fist. Her head tilts up to look at his face, directly into his eyes as his pounding fist slowly comes to rest against the glass barrier between him and her marionette hand. Breathing in deeply and sniffling through her nose, she composes herself and straightens her body. Her shoulders sink back down as the air is steadily forced out through her lips.

Silent and still aside from his racing, questioning thoughts, he waits for something, anything to come out of her mouth. He stares into her eyes that are now made even brighter by the contrast between them and the dark chords of charcoal smudged around them. The smeared makeup is an exact match of the smoky mark in the white of her right eye. Once again, tears run clouded streaks through mascara and down her pale freckled cheeks. Her head hangs, pointing her face away from his. She quickly and decisively pulls it back up, parallel with her body. His neck bends to match the motion, keeping his eyes on her face.

"I don't understand," he pleads as she looks back into his eyes.

He watches the corners of her mouth bend down involuntarily. Her fist balls up mirroring his, pressing in the same spot on the other side of the door. Her fist gives three gentle, dying taps against the glass, against his fist. The soft drumming accents each word.

"I'm. So. Sorry."

She looks back down to their hands against the glass and pushes off the door with her fist. She turns away from him and wipes her face as she walks off into the building. He waits motionless until she is completely out of sight. His hands run through his hair as he turns his back to the door and leans against it. He pushes his body off the door and runs back around the building to the chained side entrance.

171

The cord from the generator is now pulled farther into the room and is plugged into the cord from the inside of the planetarium. He pulls the door as far open as the chain will allow. He can barely make out her face in the dusky, dim, orange light of the lowest setting allowed by the control console and the lantern she carries. He knows that she is aware of his presence, but it is obvious to him that she is choosing to ignore it. The sides of his face rest against the door and the frame. Watching her through the opening, he surrenders to the conclusion that she is no longer going to acknowledge that he is there. She places the lantern on the desk at the center of the room.

His body slumps to the ground dragging his back against the grit of the cinder block wall. The door closes next to him. He leans his head against the building and reaches into his jacket pocket. He pulls a nearly empty pack of cigarettes out of the pocket. The cellophane crinkles in his hand. An orange filter jostles out of the opening as he shakes the pack. He puts it to his face, pinches the filter between his lips, and pulls the crumpled pack away, exposing the entire pathetically bent and damaged cigarette. Loosely twisted threads of tobacco threaten to fall from the sad flattened paper encasement hanging from his lips. He strikes a match and holds it to the dangling shreds of brown leaf. The match light and the tobacco kindling blaze as they touch. He squints through the glare of the torch. The sulfur fumes from the match and the generator exhaust sting his sinuses and fill his eyes with tears.

Shadows of the flame burned into his retina ghost over his view. He focuses on the spot floating against the tree line. The image is unchanged against the back of his eyelids as he forces them to close and open. He continues to blink until the glowing apparition fades. As the spot disappears from his sight, a far off strobing light replaces it, dragging his attention into the distance. Pushing himself up to his feet, he stares in awe and terror at a thin flashing line rising slowly over the entire vast edge of the horizon.

He spins and rips at the door by its handle, yanking on it as the chain rattles from the inside. He screams through the useless slit in the door.

"HEY, WHAT ARE YOU DOING? OPEN THE FUCKING DOOR!"

Holding the door open to the length of the looped chain, he looks back into the room for her. He can see the dead girl sitting at the desk. On the desk in front of her, the stack of pages he typed and the wooden tray from the floor has replaced the typewriter and lantern. She calmly holds a page from the letter out in front of her under the pin spot lamp. As she places the page she holds into the wooden tray, she picks up another page and continues to read. She glances up at him with glossy water-filled eyes. He can see her bottom lip quivering. He pounds on the outside of the door next to his face.

"STOP! SOMETHING IS HAPPENING OUT HERE. YOU…"

She wipes her eye and turns her head back to the page.

"YOU DON'T understand."

His voice lowers to nothing.

"You don't understand," he repeats to himself under his breath.

He turns back to the flashing line to see it has stretched farther into the sky. He sprints around to the front of the building to find that the line is rising from all sides, only now he can see the sky beyond the line. Past the separation, the sky cycles from day to night and back again at the pace of a blink. He can see the sun following the moon and stars as they race through the sky just beyond the line. His eyes trace down, closer to the horizon. The celestial lights stretch into luminous beams sweeping across the spectral strip of sky. Beyond the eerie lights, just above the exact point of where the sky stops and the Earth begins, the definition of the beams soften until they are lost in an empty lull of neutral, muted twilight which gradually creeps up around the atmosphere behind the chaos in front of it.

He runs back to the chained door. His entire world is now coated in the same hum as the inside of the planetarium. A low, distant, moaning rumble grows and pushes towards him from all sides making the air around him thick and stifling. He pulls at the door and tries to shout to her again, but he can no longer hear his own words, his lungs just push air into the thundering atmospheric pressure and the grind of the generator. She continues to slowly read through the pages, deliberately placing each one back into the wooden letter holder. The stack of unread pages is nearly gone.

His back turns toward the door, and he slams it closed with his body. At the farthest faded reaches of his vision, the land on the horizon is in blurred molten flux, rising and falling in a chaotic fluid motion. Hazy shapes of distant masses build and decline as they roll over themselves and rise again.

He hurries to the passenger side of the U-Haul and throws the door open. The bottles of liquor drop, shattering on the asphalt as he pulls his backpack off of the seat. His hand plunges into his bag while he runs toward the front of the building. The bag drops to the ground away from his hand, revealing the tire iron held by his white-knuckled fist. He grips the steel bar with both of his hands as he approaches the glass doors. His body turns to the side, and he swings with all of his weight. A small white dent is left in the glass. Vibrating pain swells through every bone in his hands. A splintering ache throbs up through his arms to his elbow. He pulls the iron back and swings again. The window explodes into a million falling fragments that pile up against his feet. His feet slide in the glass as he steps through the door frame.

He rushes to one of three sets of doors on a wide the curving wall that stands between him and the giant domed room. The door is locked from the inside. It doesn't budge as he tears at it with both hands. He tries each of the other two sets of doors with the same result. The handle of the final door hardly dents as he raps it repeatedly with the tire iron and shouts inaudible profanities into the now deafening roar of moving earth and crushing pressure enveloping him. Glass shards crunch beneath his feet on his way back through the broken door. The static, monochrome glow continues to grow above the horizon.

Circling back around the building, he tries to look away from the band of dizzying stellar light trails that bend around the atmosphere and cut through the sky just above the glow. The motion pulls at his eyes from his periphery. It is as irresistible and inescapable as it is nauseating. His head swims while he steadies himself against the wall next to the side door. He pulls the door back open to the length of the chain. Reaching inside, he feels the chain wrapped around the railing on the wall. A large padlock holds the chain together. He slides the links of the chain around the railing and through the inside door handle, moving the lock into the gap in the door. Holding the door with his foot, he swings the tire iron at the lock. The batted lock swings unaffected around the chain. He puts the iron into the inside door handle and pulls it against the door, pushing the wall with his foot for leverage. The handle holds firm against the prying steel bar. He pulls back from the door, turns, and throws the tire iron as far as he can. The steel bar flips through the air, silently bounces through the parking lot, and skids into the street.

His body drops to the concrete step outside of the door. The palms of his hands press into his closed eyes. His features twist and stretch with his hands grinding against them. His hands fall away from his face. He looks back out over the parking lot, the tree-lined street, and what he can see of his repaired town. A feeling of exhaustion sinks his shoulders down into his chest. His lungs heave involuntarily and his jaw pries itself open. His vision is cleared by his watering eyes. This is yawning. He is paralyzed by the realization.

The low groaning tone is now accented by high-pitched creaking and a sharp hiss. The noise draws him to his feet. He slowly wanders away from the planetarium, out into the parking lot to where he can see the leaves changing color on trees near the end of the street. The burgundy and yellow leaves on the furthest trees are falling to the ground. Through the empty writhing, growing branches, he can see the buildings on the main street beginning to crumble. The storefronts that he had repaired rapidly dilapidate into themselves. The painted surfaces gray, leaving unrecognizable rotted wood shells of the buildings he knew. The framing withers away, letting the large bay windows crash onto the sidewalks. The farthest of the warping structures fall. Their carcasses disintegrate onto the ground and drift into an approaching, swirling mass of dust.

Everything is being taken away, everything he'd done, everything that had ever been, and no one is there to even fucking care. Here is the time we stopped deserving, he thinks to himself. He can only imagine that time, after being suppressed and ignored for so long, is now unraveling through every non-moment it missed, trying to catch up to itself. His heart sinks into his stomach.

Weeds reach through crevices in the asphalt across the parking lot. The vegetation slowly takes over as the cracks widen and inch closer to where he stands. The ground beneath him shakes. He can hear life moving through the dirt under him.

He begins to feel every movement inside of himself, every muscle twitch, every throbbing pulse of dense, heavy blood coursing through every artery beneath his skin. Panic grips his chest and threatens to lock each stiffening joint in his body. His lungs painfully beg for air, not out of habit now, but out of necessity. Stomach wrenching hunger cramps his abdomen. Choking thirst collects like years of dust in his throat. His body is no longer accustomed to these archaic sensations and pangs of physical need. He realizes how much he has forgotten this satisfying torture scraping against his every nerve. It is nearly impossible for him to imagine a time when this coursing unmistakable validation of life was so commonplace that it felt like nothing, just the natural state.

Everything in him vibrates, each and every hair on his body stands on end. It is unnervingly clear to him that this is the great entitlement that is wasted on the living. Regret for his ignorance overwhelms him. How could he have been so oblivious to something that had always been there and then been so clueless as to it being gone, how long could this feeling possibly remain until it dies once again, forgotten, far away from anywhere that this primitive clenching ache of life could be appreciated?

Realizing that time will soon reach into the building, to her before he can, he backs away with a sudden start from the splitting blacktop. With each step toward the planetarium, his body falls further back into the stagnation of the Pause, shedding more of the repressed throes of mortality. He turns and stumbles, falling to the shaking ground. As his hands push him up off of the asphalt, he is sobered by the sight of his nails growing over the tips of his fingers.

He quickly jumps to his feet and takes off for the U-Haul truck. The terrifying sensation of life inside of him subsides as he climbs through the open passenger door and pushes himself into the driver's seat. He starts the truck and pulls the seatbelt around him locking it into place. The truck sways back and forth while he swings it around, reversing into the parking lot. The back tires jump over the jagged blacktop. In his side mirror, he can see that most of the town has been erased into the dust cloud. He drops the gear shift into drive and grips the steering wheel as the truck barrels toward the building, slamming the passenger door closed. The front driver's tire ramps over the knocked-over motorcycle and the curb before the passenger wheel reaches the sharp incline. The truck launches, twisting into the air. He loses his grip on the steering wheel as the front end smashes into the cinder block wall. Glancing off of the curve of the wall, the sideways truck careens away from the building. His body hangs, suspended from the lap belt against his hip. The passenger side of the truck sparks and grinds to a stop against the cement walkway surrounding the building.

Glass trickles off of him. He reaches back, grabs the steering wheel, and releases his seat belt. He holds the wheel and lets his feet drop to the scarred cement through the missing window of the passenger side door. Leaning against the dash, he slides through the empty windshield frame. As he walks around the front end of the truck, he can see into the planetarium through the crumbling cinder block wall left damaged by the crash. Pieces of crushed brick shift under his feet as he climbs through the rubble to the hole in the wall. He kicks a few cinder blocks into the room, opening the hole enough for his body to fit through it.

She is still sitting at the desk, concentrated on the final page of his letter. His mouth opens to shout to her, but his voice is silent against the roar of the chaos outside. He turns and lowers his body

180

through the hole. His feet find the railing against the wall at the bottom of the ramp, and he jumps down onto a pile of jagged, broken cinder blocks and busted drywall. He carefully navigates through the uneven debris into a clear aisle between two rows of seats.

As he looks up at her, she places the final page into the wooden letter holder. She stands from the desk, turns, and takes a few steps toward him. He stops walking as her eyes meet his. Her pale face is lined with veins of mascara. She smiles an empathetic smile of apology at him. He knows that he cannot say anything that she will hear and even if she could hear him, he has no words left to offer her.

Blood begins to drip from his brow onto his cheek. He wipes the red drop from his face and cringes at the stabbing pain of cracked ribs popping and shifting against one another as his lungs fill uncontrollably with air. He clutches his side and steadies himself with his other hand on the backrest of the seat next to him. His hand pulls him to the next seat, dragging his body through the aisle. From across the room, she watches on. She bites her lip at his obvious pain. As he steps toward her, the pain becomes more bearable. He stands up straight and looks beyond her to the other side of the planetarium.

The walls behind her and all around them are giving way to winding, stretching tree roots. Light shines in through the splitting cracks around the roots. Sections of wall fall into the building.

He focuses back on her face. She wipes her cheek with the back of her hand leaving a smeared smoky stain that matches the one in the white of her eye. He stops again, doubling over as the pain in his ribs begins to push back against his expanding lungs. As he looks back up to her, she widens her smile, and he knows this is only a mask to put him at ease. A breeze blows past him, cooling the blood on his brow. A loose red curl of her hair swings away from her cheek in the breeze and her eyes restfully close. The spinning, blurred bullet disappears. Her head sharply pushes away from her body, disjointing from her shoulders. Her hair floats, desperately reaching back to where it once hung. She is swept off of her feet and falls limply to the floor.

He drags himself through the rows of seats, moving more quickly, laboring less for breath with each step. He runs to the middle of the room. His broken ribs are only a dull cramping ache as he kneels next to her. Glossy reflective pools of blood slowly spread out away from her calm mascara smeared face. The twisted locks of her hair dampen and sink into the growing red mirror. He is distorted in the blood reflection as he leans over to lift her.

A fine red spray of blood dusts the shelves of books, the desk, typewriter, the back of the last page of his letter, and the record player on which spins a red labeled album. The brass arm rocks gently up and down as the needle glides along the grooves in the vinyl, but the music is muted amongst the discordant smothering wail of everything around him. Blood drips down over the picture of a broken record and a birthday cake on an album sleeve that leans against the player.

He gently places her onto the couch. She sinks into the worn leather, and he brushes her hair off of her face, trailing blood over her pallid, sunken cheek.

He blindly backs away from the couch and her body. His leg hits the chair behind him, tripping him into the seat at the desk. Plaster fragments and dust fall from the ceiling. Large sections of the dome fall onto the rows of seats closest to the outside wall. He can see the churning wall of dust through the gaping tears in the building. The sky shows through the skeletal framework of the ceiling. The stretched, swirling lights spin in a constricting circle around an unharmed, shrinking patch of ceiling at the center of the dome directly over him and his eroding makeshift home.

Tree roots snake toward the middle of the room through the rubble and the dust-covered rows of seats. Vines and ivy stretch over the cinder block wall ruins. As the green vegetation nears the center of the room, it is followed by a wave of brown and black decomposition leaving only ashen stains where the plants had just been. Plaster falls onto the desk in front of him. He picks up the wooden letter holder and sweeps the white residue off of the last facedown page. Blood droplets smear with the chalky residue

183

across the page.

The decaying exterior wall is swept into the cloud of dust, and he is surrounded by the riotous devastation. Chair by chair, the rows of seats fade into the cloud.

He pulls the pages from the wooden box and turns them over, placing them onto the desk. His fingertips run down the first page over the dried ink as his lungs push against his painful, shattered rib cage. He gasps for air. In his chest, his heart hammers against his sternum. Blood throbs through his veins, speeding his pulse to an erratic vibration. His hand trembles and flattens against the stack of pages as he pushes himself up, out of the chair. His back straightens against his constricting muscles. The roots reach over the couch and cover the dead girl's aged emaciating body. Atrophy weakens his stance. His knees buckle under his weight, but he steadies himself, leaning on the stack of pages. He can feel the weight of his flesh pulling at the corners of his eyes. His skin sinks away from the bones in his hands.

Through the curtain of blowing dust, he watches the shadowed blur of centuries of nature amassing and dying, falling and rebuilding against the dull sky. The vibration and heat inside of him cools and calms as his pounding heart slows. Cold, dead numbness crawls through him. With his hand on top of the letter, he tries to pull himself back up to the desk, but he can only continue to slump to the floor.

Staring into the dust-veiled confusion, he wonders what will happen after he is gone. He feels there is something. He hopes there is something. The last of the dome ceiling above him falls, completely reducing to nothing before it reaches his deteriorating hand on top of the letter. His body collapses. The weightless ash of his hand slips out of form and dissolves onto the letter. His remains are carried away into the violent unrest of time.

• • •

13. The Beginning. The Continuation. The Text.

Except for the young boy, everyone in the crowd is distracted by a commotion of dragging shoe soles chirping against the polished concrete floor. The docent's attention follows the crowd's glances over her shoulder where five security guards struggle to push two women and a man away from the exhibit. As the three detainees writhe to escape the grasp of the blue-suited men, they shout repeatedly and in unison.

"KEEP MOVING FORWARD, THE PAST IS IN THE PAST! KEEP MOVING FORWARD..."

A sixth officer passes carrying a picket sign pointed at the group of tourists. The upside-down letters read, "People are dying, here and now." The shouting quiets as the tangled cluster of limbs wrestles itself away from the crowd toward an exit door.

"You are now standing in the room where they first found The Text."

The sharp-nosed woman redirects the crowd away from the scuffle. She forces the nervous concern from her face and speaks to the boy, his father, and the group of ten people crowded around them. At his father's side, the expressionless boy peeks around the taupe curtain of a trench coat to follow her movement. Her hands fan around the glass room at the pin-light spotted items behind the thick transparent walls. Her perfectly stained red lips never actually touch one another as she recites the memorized speech through her teeth, dry from her persistent smile.

"That funny looking thing in there is called an Underwood Mechanical Typewriter. It is the machine we believe to have been used to write The Text, the oldest piece of written text known to modern society. We believe that the Underwood would still work to this very day, though no one has been allowed to touch it since the surrounding area was sealed nearly one hundred and seventy-five years ago to keep everything inside preserved. Not to mention, that it might be quite difficult to remove it from the petrified tree roots that surround it. During the Great Excavation, this room was uncovered and scanning revealed The Text perfectly sealed inside of these petrified roots."

Her hands wave to direct their attention through the clear encasement to a screen positioned over a thick, glassy, black root.

188

As the crowd's attention is diverted, her face fights to relax for a moment. The corners of her lips square off slightly, revealing anguish or exhaustion, but the change is far too subtle for anyone to notice except for the young boy peering at her from behind his father's coat.

"As you can see in the scan screen, the words on each page of The Text are clearly visible as the depth of the scan increases nanometer by nanometer, down through each page. Some people stand here for hours reading the original pages on the screen, even though I'm sure they have read it multiple times, just like the rest of us."

The boy glances at a young couple. He watches as the couple quietly argues, hatefully whispering at one another while subtly gesturing at the exhibit. The people nearest the arguing couple slide away from them, closer to the exhibit. The boy continues to watch the dispute.

"Well, I don't really give a shit what you think. I can believe what I want!"

The woman's shouted whisper is poorly timed and bursts through a quiet break in the tour guide's speech. The man throws his arms out, away from his sides, rolls his eyes, and shakes his head. The woman's eyes narrow into a disgusted scowl. She takes an obvious breath, forces her face into a polite, interested, mildly embarrassed expression, and directs her attention back to the docent and the glass encasement. The docent's eyes widen as does her painted smile, acknowledging and accepting the silent apology from the woman. A gentle tug draws the man closest to the exhibit down to the tiny face tucked into his jacket.

"Daddy, what's an Eeoode?"

Brushing the child's hair off of his forehead, the father smiles, looks back up at the exhibit, and whispers to the boy.

"It's nothing, buddy. It's just a story."

.　　　.　　　.

I'm not really even sure how any of this will get to you, if anyone will ever even read any of this, if any of this could even be useful to you, but I did it. If time starts, if it never continues, if it just ends, I wrote it and it will forever remain, written. Even if no one knows it exists, that we existed, if no one ever exists again, even if it is destroyed or lost and never found, it will always, from this point on, be something that happened. However we came to be here, we were given time to create something. I wish we had used it when we had it, maybe we would have been given more.

•   •   •

AFTERWORD

If you open your door, look out into this often heartbreaking world, and you cannot find hope or purpose, first, especially if no one else has, let me tell you that I am sorry. You have the basic human right to have some sort of happiness and satisfaction in your life and for any and every reason that you feel as though this right has been taken from you, I apologize. You are not wrong or overreacting or overly dramatic. This world is crushing and seems to be even more so every day. I do not believe that anyone with any depth of emotion or intelligence is blind to how desperate this existence has become. We all feel some amount of this even if we pretend to you that we do not.

Second, and please truly open yourself to hearing this, we all need a certain amount of help to find any hope or purpose here. Some of us are blessed by dumb luck and have someone or something that has helped us to clear a path leading straight to the realizations and understandings which satisfy our absolute need for happiness and satisfaction. Even though those of us who walk that path may never know the pain you carry, do not feel separate. The greater majority of those people who you feel could never understand you, they care more for you than you may be able to comprehend. I assure you there are far more people who do know pain, hopelessness, and purposelessness.

While no one could ever truly know exactly what it is that

you are going through, many of those people have spent their lives hoping to have an opportunity to help you find your hope and your purpose because that is where they find theirs. Let them help you, give them purpose, allow them to help you find yours, and maybe one day you can be so full of hope that you can no longer understand what it is to feel hopeless.

No one is safe from losing themselves. This is a commonality that connects us all.

If you or anyone you know is struggling with depression, talk to someone that wants to and knows how to help. Here are just a few of those people:

National Suicide Prevention Lifeline: 1-800-273-8255

National Youth Crisis Hotline: 1-800-448-4663

National Hopeline Network: 1-800-784-2433

Substance Abuse & Mental Health Services Administration:

1-800-662-4357

Crisis Text Line: Text "HOME" to 741741

If you just want to write about it and get it out of your head, email me or contact me through my social media pages. josephdnewcomer@gmail.com.

I would love to hear your thoughts.

ABOUT THE AUTHOR

Joseph D. Newcomer was born in the blue collar, Northwest Pennsylvania city of Erie in 1980. Currently, he resides in the Arizona desert with the two greatest loves of his life, his daughter, Ariella Nova and his insanely more significant other, Andrea Greenwald. He spends his time curating Ari's comic book collection while writing his next novels.

Contact Joseph at JosephDNewcomer.com.

Made in the USA
Las Vegas, NV
09 April 2021